FULFILLMENT

Hal Barwood

Reaching Up
an aspirational adventure

Fulfillment
A Finite Arts Book   v1
Published by Finite Arts LLC, Portland, Oregon

ISBN 978-0-9981914-6-1

This is a work of fiction. Marin County California, the City of Novato, the National Security Agency, game developers, hackers, cyber attacks, and cynical employees are all real; but the locations, communities, and enterprises depicted herein are either fictional in themselves or fictional in detail. All the characters and incidents in this fictional world are products of the author's imagination. No resemblance to any real person is intended, and no actual hacking tricks are revealed.

Acknowledgments . . .

Many thanks to the readers willing to read unfinished versions of this tale: Barbara, Jonathan, & Tobias Barwood; Betsy & Curt Blanchard; Robert Dalva, Louis Castle, Beverly Graves, and Tony Hsieh.

Thanks always to Google, Wikipedia, and the rest of the World Wide Web for demonstrating so vividly, so regularly, so clearly, that life has more answers than questions, a lot of them wrong.

About the Author . . .

Hal Barwood is a veteran writer with multiple credits in multiple media. Find out more here . . .

www.finitearts.com

with nostalgic affection for . . .

Adam, Aric, Bill, Brian, Bob, Chris, Christy, Clint, Collette, Darragh, Dave, Dave, Dave, Derek, Don, Eric, Gary, Geoff, Geoff, Gordon, Graham, Greg, Harley, Joe, Jon, Josef, Lee, Lou, Lynne, Mai, Mark, Matt, Michael, Michelle, Mike, Mike, Mike, Nick, Nicole, Noah, Pat, Paul, Peter, Randy, Raph, Reed, Reeve, Ron, Sean, Seth, Steve, Steve, Steve, Tim, Tim, Tim, Tom, Tony, Vince, Wayne, William, Yoko

. . . fellow developers all

Table of Contents

>>> 0001

PART ONE

1
00000001

"Promise me, Ollie . . . promise me you won't get involved with those awful video games."

Oliver Page sucked in a deep breath.

"I won't do anything without giving it a lot of thought, Gram."

Page had recently graduated *magna cum laude* from Camberwell College, a well-regarded local school not far from his house on leafy Kosciuszko Avenue in the Wicker Park area of Chicago. The ten-stop trip on the Blue Line train was about as far as he had ever been from home. He desperately wanted to see more of the world, but he didn't have the heart to tell his ailing grandmother, who housed and guided him all through his school years, that he had already accepted a programming job at *Brass Knuckles Mobility,* a developer of casual role-playing games in San Rafael, California.

Here's how it happened:

When Page was ten his father took him to see a re-release of *Star Wars.* The experience set Page's mind ablaze and etched itself permanently into his consciousness, something not lost on his parents, who fostered his interest in that faraway galaxy with an unusual Christmas present a few months later: Kenner Products Item No. 69370, a collectible plastic statue of *YODA The Jedi Master.* The blurb on the worn cardboard box declared, *He Answers All Your Questions.*

Page discovered that he could ask a question — any question at all — and when he inverted the little five-inch statue, Yoda's answer would appear, offering cryptic advice. The statue was, in fact, a merchandising knock-off of the popular *Magic 8-Ball* toy. It delivered the same twenty answers, ten positive, five ambiguous, five negative, but now expressed in Yoda's fractured grammar. The statue's pronouncements were all embossed on the triangular faces of a twenty-sided icosahedron that floated up on demand from the depths of an inky fluid.

His first inquiries provoked answers that seemed uncanny to a naïve ten-year-old. The little Jedi's apparent insight made the hair stand up on Page's arms and neck. The boy was outwardly shy and timid, and his parents worried about it, but deep inside he felt bold, because he was blessed with an invaluable guide to life's perplexities . . . *Magic Yoda.*

Years later, when it came time for Page to select a college, he consulted the little plastic oracle. His family could just barely afford the tuition and fees of a private school, but only a local one.

Mother and grandmother wanted him to enroll at DeVry. He himself leaned toward Camberwell, where the program allowed for a heady mixture of liberal and technical training.

"Should I go to DeVry, keep Mom happy?" he wondered. Yoda's upside-down response read:

IT CANNOT BE, NO

A decisive answer . . . and it sent him off to Camberwell.

Five years later (it took that long to get all his classes and earn enough credits to graduate) Page faced another dilemma. In the final months of the school year he sent out dozens of resumés advertising his computer chops. His degree was in the ambitiously entitled Haptic Design track. Not exactly computer science, but the courses gave him the chance to learn a thing or two about computers, about the software that runs them, and allowed him to master the Unity Technologies Content Creation Engine in the process.

Only two companies responded to his inquisitive flurry. One was Web Weavers, a Chicago internet design firm, and the other was Brass Knuckles. The West Coast was magnetically attractive, but the prospect of leaving the comfort of his childhood habitat filled him with nameless dread.

"Should I head for California?" queried Page doubtfully.

He was no longer talking to a little Yoda toy. Having learned from his college teachers about the perils of copyright infringement, he created his own fictional mentor — *Master Ming* — who appeared as an Asian wizard dwelling in a clever *chatbot app* he programmed in his computer science class.

Page was casually acquainted with another dispenser of enigmatic wisdom, the *I Ching,* which inspired him to fashion the wizard's advisories in the style of that ancient *Book of Changes,* thus:

THE SUPERIOR MAN STRIDES FORWARD

Indirect perhaps, but clear enough to decide the issue.

Cheered on by the chatbot's poetic response, Page began to anticipate his forthcoming adventure. He sat down and watched *Singin' in the Rain, La La Land,* and *The Graduate* twice each. He spent hours in bookstores collecting paper maps and travel guides.

His mother, anticipating the end of her son's drain on family finances, happily elevated the spending limit on his credit card to the princely sum of $5,000. His stepfather, pleased to see a glimmer of initiative in the boy, signed over Mom's aging Honda Accord (after upgrading her own ride to a fancy new Lexus).

Now Page was ready to travel, and the time came to say goodbye. That, and the delicate business of informing his lonely grandmother of his exotic plans without alarming or inflaming her. His imminent departure made him feel guilty, as if leaving her care was a betrayal. On the other hand, he suspected that Gram's recent health problems were a ploy to gain sympathy and tie him to her apron strings, an accusatory thought he would never dare to express aloud.

Instead he stood respectfully at her bedside and mumbled lame notions of scratching an exploration itch before returning and settling down right in the middle of good old Wicker Park.

"I know you like to fiddle around with those computers and those damn phones everybody has now, but you take care, that stuff is no substitute for real people in the real world," said the old lady, lying on her back, aiming her words at the ceiling.

"True, Gram. I hear you. But that's what I studied at school, remember?"

"Yes I do. I talked to your mother and that boyfriend of hers, but they don't give a damn about you, so they're no help to me."

"I know, I know. They got married, by the way."

"So they say. They're playing golf out there in Denver. You can visit them as you whiz through mile-high country."

"I could do that. I might. We'll see."

"California? Why not the Moon? I'll never see you again."

"Come on, Gram, I'll be back."

"Don't try to humor me, young man. In spite of your diploma, you don't know a thing about anything, so listen. Wherever you end up, never pay more than twenty-five percent of your income for rent, understood?"

"Twenty-five percent. Got it."

"Find some friends who know their way around."

"Friends, unh-huh, will do."

"Change your oil. Do that and your mother's car will run forever. And rotate your tires."

"Oil, tires, yup."

Gram lifted her arms, pushed against the headboard of her bed, and sat herself up. Her face was pale.

"Whoa, you okay?"

"I'll be fine. Now here's something else. You didn't go to your senior prom in high school."

"Nope, didn't."

"Did you ever go to a mixer, or a dance, or a party up there in Camberland?"

"Can't say I did." He shook his head. "Nope. That always seemed like a fraternity and dorm kind of thing. Not for me."

Gram cocked her head. She studied her grandson, noting his regular features; his piercing blue eyes, his lanky frame, his upright posture . . . and his contrasting awkward demeanor.

"You're a good-looking kid. You like girls?"

"I guess."

"You guess?" She scowled. "What — is it boys?"

Page blushed to the roots of his light brown hair. "God, no. Girls are okay by me."

"You have never had a date, have you?"

Page squirmed.

"Nope. Not yet."

"Oh my stars. You want to grow up, right?"

Page was five feet ten inches tall. "I'm pretty well grown, Gram."

The woman snorted. "You know what I'm talking about. Birds. Bees. A date. Something to try out there in California, where no one you know will witness your mistakes."

"That's very encouraging, Gram."

2
00000010

Having faithfully dispatched his filial duties, Page threw his clothes into a wheelie suitcase from Ross Dress For Less, gassed up his mother's old Honda, and rolled onto westbound Interstate 80. California, here I come.

```
DAY ONE:
Arrive Council Bluffs Iowa
(Missouri River / Omaha Nebraska)
446 miles on the clock
Dinner at Perkins Family Restaurant — $16
Overnight at Motel 6 — $50
```

Page wrote the information down on his laptop. He thought it wise to keep a log as a memento of his personal odyssey and a tally of his expenses. He was on a very tight budget.

As he settled into bed his eyes were wide. The motel he found on the internet turned out to be located smack in the middle of an industrial transportation complex. Headlight beams swept across the curtains of his room at all hours. The growl of heavy-duty diesel engines, the whine of fifteen-speed transmissions, and the thumping roar of compression release Jake brakes made sleep intermittent.

He reflected restlessly on this first day. He was now hundreds of miles farther from home than he had ever traveled. He felt unsure of himself, felt lost, felt small in the vastness of America's broad plains. A tremendous wave of nostalgia for his grandmother's sharp tongue and the comfort of her house washed over him.

"This job better pan out, or it's back Chicago," he vowed.

▼

Page woke up late. His itinerary called for another westbound segment of I-80, ending up in Cheyenne, Wyoming, five hundred and seventy-six miles farther west. But his nighttime anxiety had been erased by bright sunshine, a cloudless blue sky, and the waffle machine in the motel's breakfast nook. His sense of adventure revived, and endless miles on the Interstate no longer seemed all that adventurous. He remembered his fondness for the movie *Close Encounters of the Third Kind* and realized that a visit to Devil's Tower, the fictional marker of humanity's first contact with aliens, was well within reach. Oh, and he could take a look at patriotic Mount Rushmore on the way there.

He had given himself nine days to reach the Bay Area of California. If he stayed on I-80 he could get there in five. Too easy. When he started munching his waffle he was set on the excursion. By the last bite he was vacillating. Who knew what travel conditions would be like in the middle of nowhere? The map on his laptop showed a lot of squiggly lines where the roads were drawn. Maybe he should re-think, save the adventure for another trip after he was well-established professionally. Right.

Then again, maybe he was being foolishly cautious. Only one way to resolve the problem: Master Ming.

"Should I change my route and go see Devil's Tower?" Page asked aloud and pressed a key on his laptop. Other motel patrons looked up from their breakfast muffins and coffee. They stared as Ming appeared on the computer screen. The virtual wizard's answer was displayed below his image in large type:

A PETTY MAN GOES NOWHERE

"Ouch, that hurts. Come on, I need advice. So again: Devil's Tower? Should I go?"

Another keypress produced a different response:

THE WIND IS FAVORABLE

"All right, much better. What I wanted to know!"

Page was strangely elated by the outcome of his little séance. He turned his Honda onto Interstate 29 and headed north toward South Dakota.

```
DAY TWO:
Arrive Rapid City South Dakota
526 miles
Hey — Mountain Time Zone!
Dinner at Millstone Family Restaurant — $12
Overnight at Ramada Inn Rapid City — $67
```

The motel bed was king size. He sprawled out while still in his clothes and slept for nine hours.

▼

After breakfast he detoured to the southwest, marveling at the Black Hills rising so suddenly out of the plains, and spent half an hour at the Mount Rushmore National Memorial. He was goggle-eyed at Gutzon Borglum's immense granite heads peering into the distance from their lofty heights. He had once seen the movie *North by Northwest* and imagined Cary Grant sliding down George Washington's shoulder. The idea made him shudder.

He was skeptical about Teddy Roosevelt's place among the greats, however, and was appalled to learn that the project wasn't inspired by patriots, but by cynical promoters bent on luring outsiders to the remote state of South Dakota. It worked. Two million tourists visited the site annually. Now he was one of them.

▼

By midafternoon he had navigated I-90, US Highway 14, and Wyoming Highway 24 to Devils Tower National Monument, a few miles north of Carlile Junction, following the twisty little line on his smartphone map.

The ancient volcanic plug soaring above him looked just like Roy Neary's speculative sculpture pieces in *Close Encounters.* Tall, lonely, mysterious, forbidding . . . alien.

What really captured his attention was the unexpected prairie dog town, as exotic to a Chicago lad as the plains of Africa. He spent twenty minutes with half a dozen other tourists standing as still as possible while waiting for the cute little rodents to pop up and show themselves. When they finally did, a woman clapped her hands, and they all disappeared again.

```
DAY THREE:
Arrive Gillette Wyoming
218 miles
Dinner at Pizza Hut — $9
Overnight at Super 8 Motel — $38
```

▼

Page identified one more iconic American attraction on his way west: Yellowstone, the world's first national park.

When he arrived at the visitor center near Old Faithful, a sign told him that the next eruption would occur in ninety-one minutes.

He moseyed out to the circular patch of bare ground sterilized by the geyser's sulfurous waters and sat down in the gallery to await events. Steam rose irregularly in puffs and wafted away on a light breeze, encouraging vigilance. But being faithful, he soon learned, was a relative kind of thing. One hundred and thirty-nine minutes elapsed before water finally spewed forth with much wheezing and gurgling. The display reminded him of a giant whale surfacing for air after a long dive.

He was tired and bored, and his butt hurt from the hard seating. He began to wonder if he had made a small mistake; if dodging south to float in the buoyant waters of the Great Salt Lake would have been a better idea, and maybe see where the historic Golden Spike was driven to establish the world's first continental railroad.

Too late now.

```
DAY FOUR:
Arrive Idaho Falls / Snake River / Idaho
453 miles
Dinner at Denny's — $15
Overnight at Fairbridge Inn and Suites — $63
```

Page drove into town after dark. Just before crossing the river he passed by the Idaho National Laboratory. Lights were blazing in the byzantine complex of low buildings and bulging domes. He had read about the place. Somewhere inside, he knew, alchemists in white coats were busy inventing novel ways to turn the nuclear reactions of base uranium into electric power gold.

Wow — he imagined becoming radioactive. When he turned off the lights in his room he checked to be sure that his skin didn't glow.

▼

A waffle in the morning.

Page was becoming addicted to these do-it-yourself breakfast items, which were a major feature of the cheap motels he favored.

On the way out of town he steered his Honda into a Sinclair gas station, taking a chance on the odd brand, because the company's logo was reinforced at the curb by a green dinosaur statue that rose twenty feet into the air. He snapped a selfie standing in front of the thing and texted the result back to Gram.

Once the image was winging its way across country to demonstrate his good health and safety, Page filled the gas tank, cleaned the windshield, checked the tires, and set out once again on President Eisenhower's great gift to mobility, the Interstate highway system.

First, I-15 to Pocatello, then I-86 and I-84 to Twin Falls. There he turned south onto US 93, the Great Basin Highway, and followed it to Wells, Nevada, where he rejoined the Interstate.

Now, on westbound I-80, Page was driving through high desert terrain, and he could see for thirty miles in all directions. Mountain peaks, blue in the hazy distance, lifted up the horizon. The effect on a sheltered child of Chicago was profound. The view was intoxicating; it sent chills up his spine. It was here, in the vast open spaces of Nevada, that his first doubts about returning to live in the East occurred.

```
DAY FIVE:
Arrive Winnemucca Nevada
(Humboldt River / Goes nowhere!)
446 Miles
Pacific Time — get used to this!
Dinner at La Tortilla Factory — $11
Overnight at Days Inn — $61
```

Page had barely heard of tacos back in Chicago, where Polish sausages were king, but he saw a lot of signs advertising them on the current leg of his trip and got to wondering about Mexican cuisine, which he guessed would be unavoidable in California. La Tortilla Factory, around the corner from his motel, did a good job of satisfying his curiosity. He wasn't sold on the crackly corn shells folded around beef and chicken, but now he was familiar with one of the West's signature food items. When the waitress brought the bill, he asked about the green glob on his plate and learned all about avocados and guacamole. People eat this stuff?

He was ready for bed, but also curious about the darker side of Nevada — gambling. He was especially curious about the effect of random number generators on software-driven slot machine payoffs. It was an outgrowth of his personal obsession with Master Ming and Ming's pseudo-randomly presented answers to life's burning questions.

A waxing Moon was rising when he set out from his motel on foot. It was ten blocks along West 4th Street to Parker's Model T Casino, and he hiked the distance to get a feel for the dry air of a hot desert evening.

Inside, flanked by an authentically restored 1918 Ford Model T pickup truck, were ranks of glittering slot machines. Sullen older women wearing baggy shorts and wizened ranchers in checkered shirts were silently glued to their unwholesome habits. Cigarette smoke filled the air. He grimaced, purchased a $10 ticket, and gave the *Gunslinger Gal* video slot a try. He was comfortable staring at the glowing screen, since modern gambling devices were a branch of video game technology, distant cousins of the shooters and role-playing games on his laptop and smartphone. Aside from the noxious air and the age of the other players, the casino itself resembled the arcades of his youth.

However, after three virtual 'spins' he was down to the last dollar on his ticket. His opinion of casino entertainment sank low. But then his fortunes changed. On his next try, three busty saloon gals popped up on the payline, then three horse heads. Finally, three rootin'-tootin' cowboys with drawn guns lit racer lights and rang bells. He floated off his stool some twenty-five bucks ahead of the game. He was a winner.

Randomness, how very mysterious. He silently vowed never to gamble again.

▼

Over a morning waffle and bad coffee, he traced his route to the Bay Area on his laptop. Hmm, less than five hundred miles, and all on wide-open I-80. He concluded that his destination was now within reach and dispatched an email to Brass Knuckles, letting them know that, barring a traffic accident, he would show up on their doorstep next day.

Then it was back onto I-80 and a brown landscape blurring past the windows of his Honda.

He shot through Reno without a stopover, keeping his eyes on the Sierra Nevada mountain range, a high wall of snow-capped granite looming ahead. As the road angled upward, he tried to understand how any work of man could penetrate the vertical shafts of stone that confronted him. The Donner party misfortunes crossed his mind. But then the road bent southward, and he noticed the Truckee River running beside the highway. The mountainside wasn't vertical after all, and Interstate 80 was rising on the water grade. Halfway up the slope he crossed the border. He was now in California, in the Golden State.

He let out a whoop.

In another half hour the harsh desert was behind him, and he rolled into the town of Truckee itself. There he detoured south to Tahoe City, following the river to its source, Lake Tahoe.

He just had to see the world-famous lake. As he neared, tall trees crowded around the road, then gave way to a thirty mile stretch of deep blue water. The summer air at 6,000 feet was crystal clear, and the far shore was sharp in the distance. Not as big as Lake Michigan, whose far shore was out of sight, but Tahoe, nestled among towering mountain crags, easily won the scenery contest.

Later in the afternoon, while descending into the suburbs of Sacramento, Page caught a glimpse of his first palm trees, tropical fantasies promising deliverance from the miseries of wintertime Chicago. A larger doubt about returning there tickled his impressionable brain.

By nightfall he was nearing the outer edge of the sprawling San Francisco Bay Area, and traffic slowed.

He joined a long line of commuters slowing and going through the outer suburbs, already more populous than any city he had passed through on his trip. The slow pace gave him plenty of time to stare at Six Flags Discovery Park, a jungle of twisting steel roller coasters and other demonically inspired thrill rides. It looked dead on a weekday.

```
DAY SIX:
Arrive Vallejo California — !
(Bay Area)
Dinner at Denny's — $11
Overnight at Motel 6 Vallejo Six Flags West — $76
```

After downing his Philly Cheesesteak Omelette at Denny's, Page sat down at the tiny desk in his motel and conscientiously tallied up the cost of his journey:

```
Motels — $355
Lunch and dinner — $125
Gas for Honda — 96 gal @ $2.50/gal = $240
Taxes — $50 (approximate)
Total = $770
```

And all this on his credit card! Whew . . . just over $4000 left. The outflow of money he didn't yet have in his pocket gave him the willies. He shook off humiliating visions of bankruptcy and spent the rest of the evening leafing through his thumb-worn paperback copy of *Unity for U,* his favorite tutorial on the Unity software development system. He was intent on reviewing C# computer language syntax, boning up for the big day tomorrow.

3
00000011

"Welcome to Brass Knuckles," said a heavy thirtyish woman, when Page knocked hesitantly on the company's office door in San Rafael just shy of the noon hour. He was late, having deliberately waited for morning commute traffic through Marin County, a sprawling suburb on the north side of San Francisco Bay, to subside.

The woman was wearing a bulky maroon sweatshirt over black tights. She noted his button-down shirt and his chinos and smiled. "You must be Page. That *is* you, our new programmer, right?"

Page pointed at his chest. "Uh, yes, ma'am, that's me. Ollie."

"Well hooray. Now we might actually ship our game on time." She grabbed his hand and gave it a vigorous shake.

"I'm Karen Hoffman, I herd the cats."

"Beg pardon?"

"I do the Lord Donald's bidding."

"What?"

"I'm the producer. Also the main artist and occasional 3D modeler." She swept back a mane of dark hair and pushed a pair of purple-framed glasses onto her forehead. "Here, let's meet the boss. Then it's paperwork."

Brass Knuckles Mobility's spartan offices occupied half the second floor of a nondescript wood-framed commercial building on Paul Drive, nestled between Fairbanks Plumbing and Rick's Auto Glass. The location, disguised by leafy trees and shrubs, was part of a large industrial complex just off busy US 101, the Redwood Highway, fifteen miles north of the Golden Gate Bridge in the Terra Linda section of San Rafael.

Donald Bakstrom, the CEO and owner of the company, occupied a tiny office in one corner. Hoffman politely knocked on the open door and led Page inside.

"Hey, Don. Here he is — our new hire, Oliver Page."

"Ollie," amended Page.

Bakstrom reached out and shook Page's hand with genial detachment. The CEO was forty-five, slim, athletic, near-sighted, a generation older than Page. He was wearing a white golf shirt, khaki shorts and yellow-tinted glasses.

"So — Ollie — why game development? What brought you to our door?"

Page had never put his motives into words before, and Bakstrom's question threw him.

"I dunno exactly. Hard to explain. But . . . I played your last game, *Sword,* for hours and hours."

Bakstrom grinned. "Hard to explain being crazy, yeah?" He sprang from behind his desk. "Come on, I'll show you around."

There wasn't much to see. Beige cubicle walls separated half a dozen desks purchased from Ikea, behind which sat employees not much older than himself. They waved as Bakstrom pointed to each one.

"Michael, Ashok, Peter, Ralph, James . . ."

Page waved back. Bakstrom smiled and gestured toward Hoffman.

"And Karen, our token woman. You already met."

Page rocked back on his heels. Hoffman suppressed a frown.

Bakstrom didn't seem to notice their reactions. "Here's your cube," he said, indicating the last desk.

Page surveyed his new professional home. Papers everywhere, coffee rings on the papers and on the desk itself. A 3D printed statue of buxom Lara Croft behind the computer keyboard. Sticky notes plastered on the cubby walls.

"Great to have you join us," said Bakstrom. "Going to make a big difference around here, I know." He tapped Page on the shoulder, invited him to sit with an outstretched hand, then abruptly spun on his heel and returned to his office.

"See, the reason we hired you is him — the guy who used to sit here," said Hoffman by way of explaining the desktop mess.

"Oh?"

"Trevor. He was our main engine guy. Fantastic talent. But he left. Working for Uber now, optimizing their driver database."

"Mmm, Trevor . . ."

"So we decided to convert everything to Unity."

"Unh-huh, not a bad idea."

"And that's where you come in — you're the converter."

Page's face turned pale. He had worked with Unity, built a few apps, but he didn't try to fool himself. He was no expert.

Hoffman clocked his sudden pallor. "You're familiar with Unity, right? That's what your resumé said."

"I'm no expert," he confessed, pitching his voice to feign nonchalance.

Hoffman shrugged. "How hard can it be? We're building a dinky little session RPG for iOS and Android. It's not even real 3D."

Page nodded, nodded several times while he gathered his wits. "Right. I'll be fine. Unity, great."

"Okay, then, I'll bring the employment agreement, IRS crap and so forth. Scribble something coherent and then . . . lunch."

▼

"So here's the deal," said Hoffman between bites of her BLT on whole wheat. They were sitting in Dick's Diner, on the frontage road a few blocks from the studio.

"I have booked you into the Verdugo Inn on Lincoln for the night. It's expensive, but tomorrow, unless you've got something else in mind, I found a nice little room in Fairfax."

"Nice?"

"That means cheap. Here in Marin where rents are to the moon, that's important."

"Oh, got it."

"It'll be good for the duration."

Page was swimming in ignorant confusion. He thought he had just detected a termination date for his employment lurking among various company management secrets.

"Duration — ?"

"You know — just out of school, first job, mountain of student debt, no idea what you're doing, right?"

"Oh yeah, for sure."

"Been there, dude. After a few paychecks, the dizziness will go away, we'll ship — that's bigger than big — you'll get a feather in your cap, and hey, then you're a vet — you survived."

Page started to relax. His breezy new boss seemed genuinely friendly. He thought she could lose a pound or two, but he also thought she was okay, and he hoped nothing would happen to change his opinion.

"So, newbie," continued Hoffman, raising her head for a good look at her naïve lunch companion. "What's your goal in life? Our CEO didn't get an answer. I want one. What's your five-year plan?"

Page froze.

"Is this like an interview question?"

Hoffman smiled.

"You're hired already. I'm just curious. The ox presents its head to the ax. Can't help wondering why . . ."

"And yet, you're here, in the biz, right?"

"Some of us just can't help ourselves."

"Sounds like me."

"Another lost soul then. So tell me . . . what's driving you?"

Page fooled around with the onion rings that came with his lunch. He was reluctant to discuss his ambitions.

"Well, if you must know, it's pretty simple . . ."

He bit into his sandwich and chewed thoughtfully while he forced himself to search for the right words.

". . . I want a game with my name on it."

Hoffman ignored Page's discomfort and nodded approval.

"Good answer. Might not happen at Brass Knuckles, though. You all right with that?"

Page shrugged acceptance and changed the subject to get past the awkward moment.

"You know, driving in, I missed the exit and had to turn around near the pink flying saucer building down the road. What is that thing?"

"Marin County Civic Center. Frank Lloyd Wright's last opus."

"Really. There's a lot of his stuff in Chicago, where I grew up."

"This one is from his science-fiction period."

"The crazy blue roof, the gold tower." Page shook his head in wonderment.

"Looks like an antenna, right? I think that's how the County Board of Supervisors talk to Flash Gordon when they need advice."

"Wow, here I am on Planet Mongo."

Hoffman smiled.

"Feels like it sometimes."

Back in the office Page tore all the sticky notes off his cubby wall. He fetched a damp paper towel from the grimy kitchenette and scoured the desk free of coffee stains. Then he piled up the papers scattered everywhere. Some of them made reference to code modules, asset management, version control.

While he studied these documents the dark-haired young man in the next cube leaned over the wall.

"You're Oliver Page, right? That's your name?"

"Everyone calls me Ollie."

"Ollie, whoa, that's terrific. I'm Jimmy Fillmore."

He stuck out a fist. Page reached up and bumped it.

"You're the Unity guy," continued Fillmore. His dark brown eyes were darting restlessly here and there.

"I guess so. How about yourself? What are you working on?"

"Just about everything. Tools, collision detection, player sync, serializing the savegames."

"Sounds like heavy lifting," said Page.

"Nahh, for this game? Fucking *Shrine of the Spear?* Easy-peasy."

Page nodded robotically. He didn't know if the game was easy to build or not.

"Well, what about my code?" queried Fillmore.

"What are you writing? C++?"

"Pretty much."

"We'll need to convert everything to C#, unless I find a way to hook in your stuff via something in the Asset Store."

"Shit."

"I know. More work for both of us."

"Welcome to the jungle, bro."

"Unh-huh."

"And word to the wise — just ignore everything The Donald tells you. He's a moron, doesn't know C from Shinola."

This piece of advice disturbed Page. "But he's the designer, right? Wasn't *Shrine of the Sword* a big hit?"

"We got lucky last time. Bakstrom knocked *Sword* off *Crisis Directive Two.* Gave it a fantasy vibe. Don't quote me, but on his own the man couldn't design wallpaper."

Page was prepared to admire his new company and its owner. He was shocked to hear Fillmore's harsh assessment.

"Mum's the word," he mumbled.

4
00000100

Page's room in Fairfax was on the second floor of an aging stucco building hard by Sir Francis Drake Boulevard, one of the main commuter arteries between rural West Marin and the bustling commercial enterprises of San Anselmo, San Rafael, Larkspur, Corte Madera, and southern Novato. It was narrow, with just enough room for a small desk and one twin bed. The only window looked out onto the street. Traffic noise was constant, a twenty-four-hour annoyance.

The room was equipped with a tiny two-cubic-foot refrigerator, a microwave oven, and a hot plate. The bathroom and its antique shower were down the hall, used by five different residents. Altogether, the arrangements were less than ideal. Disgusting, actually. To Page, it seemed like he was back in college, in one of the dorms he visited when friends staged a beer party.

And cheap? Hang on. The rent was $1000 per month.

Luckily, his projected yearly salary of $45,000 — not bad for a first job, really — worked out to around $850 per week, and the deficit in his credit card account was soon erased.

Although his living quarters were bleak, he hardly noticed, because he spent little time in them. For one hundred and twenty consecutive days following his first knock on the Brass Knuckles door, he spent almost every waking hour in his cubicle converting code modules and art assets to work within the Unity framework.

"Okay, Jimmy. Here's what we do," said Page on his ninth day at work, when he first realized that the innumerable Herculean tasks involved in getting *Shrine of the Spear* into shape would be his curse. He, Oliver Page, the new kid in town, was destined to clean the Augean stables of the endless software revisions, last-minute features, and ridiculous bugs that kept cropping up as the team digested the project. He was most definitely in deep shit.

"Jimmy? You there?"

Fillmore put down the controller he was using to play *Toad Wars* on his computer. He leaned over the cubby wall. "Yeah?"

"We bundle your C++ in a plain C wrapper, and I write a C# script that calls your functions like we've got a library."

"I don't have to re-write?"

"No, you don't. Well, mostly not. Maybe a little tweaking."

Like many people at age twenty-one, Page did not know himself very well when he started at Brass Knuckles, his first real job. Now he was slowly discovering that he had what it takes. His grip on Unity proved to be firm and professional, and since none of his co-workers had the slightest inkling, he became the acknowledged company guru from the get-go. It gave him a modicum of personal confidence. It showed.

Hoffman, fearing the worst from the shy kid, was relieved. Fillmore was overjoyed. His code — 175,000 lines worth — was painfully composed in the flexible, recondite, mind-numbing C++ computer language over many months. Having it ported into the new engine with little effort left him plenty of time for sidebar projects, goofing off, and leveling up his avatars in half a dozen massive multiplayer online games.

Page had pulled all-nighters in college, but those labors, although occasionally intense, were brief. After the first month toiling without a break, his waking hours were spent in a fog, and he was perpetually exhausted. But he also felt a peculiar strength, buoyed up by the discovery that working hard for long hours was his personal superpower.

▼

"So, no overtime, no overtime pay."

Page already knew, but he and Fillmore were taking a long lunch break to celebrate *Alpha*, and he wanted to gripe.

"Nope. California law allows us slaves to be called managers, working on salary at our own direction. We're exempt."

"That sucks. The way we're going, I should be rich."

"Ha ha, that's funny. Nobody gets rich here, except maybe Donnie-boy."

"Right, we just get pizza on Sundays."

"What a perk, huh?"

Page nodded grim agreement. He had been on the job for just a few months, but the novelty of game development had long since worn off. Now, like an old hand, he was becoming cynical.

"Theoretically, all the elements are in," he noted. "Alpha, right? The game is running. I'm spearing goblins on my smartphone. So what's up with Ralph's dialogue? He's got a new version every day."

"Don's orders. Death from above."

Page sighed. "Ashok is still revving levels."

"He is the bugmeister."

"And I have to clean up every rev."

Fillmore gave him a sidelong look. "That's not all you're doing. I see another game on your screen in between our frantic builds. What are you up to when you're not zapping bugs?"

"Oh nothing, really." Page was mortified to be called for wasting company time. He touched his forehead. "Working on a chatbot."

"No, no, I saw a game. Little aliens running around."

"You mean my swarm. It's just a way to work on my Unity skills."

"It looked pretty interesting. I'd like to play it."

Page hauled out his smartphone and handed it to Fillmore. "It's in my sandbox. Tap to dodge the slimy horde."

Fillmore spent a few minutes engrossed in the half-finished app.

When he handed the phone back, his expression indicated new respect. "Don't let Don see this."

"Why not?"

"He'll steal it."

▼

At Halloween, the team reached *Beta*. A select group of outsiders was now allowed to play the game and offer feedback. The team took a lot of heat. Bakstrom read everyone the riot act.

Hoffman took Fillmore and Page to lunch at Dick's Diner.

"Don is canceling the selfie feature," she announced.

"You're kidding. I love that feature," said Page.

"You ask me, it's the best part of the damn game. The only original part," added Fillmore.

"That's because you designed it, big boy."

"So?"

"So here we are almost ready to go, and we're still struggling with the AR, getting game characters to appear beside our players in the photos they take."

"Fucking augmented reality. I'll make it happen, don't worry," vowed Fillmore.

"No, you won't," growled Hoffman. "It's out. Don's orders. We need to ship this turkey." She rose from the table. "Excuse me while I powder my nose."

Page watched her toddle off to the women's restroom.

"Hey, Jimmy — what should I do? Karen's been giving me the eye."

"She what? You? What makes you thinks so?"

"She's been looking at me."

"You're imagining things, dude."

"No, I'm not. The eye. She eyeballs me. Does she want me to ask her out?"

"What are you talking about?"

"I don't know how to do it. You know . . . ask."

"Don't worry about it."

"And what if I don't want to, anyway? She's not exactly my type."

"Your *type?* Listen to you! Have you ever *in your life* asked anyone out? Coffee? Dinner? Movie?"

"Nope. Got me."

"So don't start now, okay?"

At that moment Hoffman returned to the table. She picked up her purse, leaned over, and kissed Fillmore lightly on the cheek.

"Okay, guys, gotta do some shopping. See you back at the ranch."

Page watched her exit the restaurant. Fillmore was small, and Hoffman was large. The combination baffled him.

"Oops, sorry about that. I had no idea," he said, raising his hands in a surrender gesture and blushing crimson.

"None, obviously. I put it down to overwork."

▼

In early November the team sat down together and went through a long check list. Code? Woohoo, it's complete. A-bugs? None open that would stop players from finishing the game. B-bugs? None open that would make the game look amateurish. C-bugs? Thirteen still open, encapsulating a debate on tiny look-and-feel issues that was never going to get resolved.

"That's it! Tonight we build our first *Golden Master Candidate,*" Hoffman declared. "The iOS version."

A week later, Apple accepted the submission. By then the Android version, with its provisions for a dozen different screen shapes and resolutions, was clean enough to ship as well.

By Thanksgiving, the Nintendo DS version was also finished, wrapping up the project.

▼

Page took three days off to upgrade his Master Ming app. He was concerned about the stupid pseudo-random number generator he was using to pick the wizard's cryptic answers. It wasn't much more than getting milliseconds off his computer's internal clock; good enough for college work, but he saw clumps when he ran a scatter plot.

More alarming was news about Russian hackers cracking the random number generators in Las Vegas video slots for big payoffs, and he certainly didn't want Russians meddling with answers to any of his important personal questions.

So, using his modest computer science knowledge and a good set of Google search terms, he set about constructing some decent randomizing code in JavaScript, the computer language of the World Wide Web. Here's the methodology he used:

First, pick a *seed* with some oddball magic number to start the process, like this:

```
var seed = 1238473661;
```

Next, create a *function* to twiddle the hell out of the seed number:

```
function rolldice(seed){
    seed = seed * 16807 % 2147483647;
    return seed/2147483647;
};
```

Once that's done, *call* the function:

```
var s = rolldice(seed);
var r = s;
```

Now *crunch* the result down to pick one of Ming's twenty possible answers:

```
r *= 100;
r = Math.trunc(y);
r = Math.floor(y * 0.2);
```

And then the final, most important step — *renew the seed* with the current output, which is how the twiddling function makes the following results unpredictable :

```
seed = (Math.trunc(s * 2147483647));
```

Of course, he didn't actually create the function. Instead, he fooled around with the well-known Park-Miller algorithm and modified that. He was enchanted by the way his simple chunk of code produced such wonderfully different numbers each time it ran. Random, or almost.

He also contemplated the Jackstraw algorithm as an adult alternative to his do-it-yourself mod, but he didn't understand its complexities, so he rejected it and studied Lord Ming's actual answers instead. One defect bothered him above all others: in none of his twenty responses did the crotchety old soul suggest *direct action*.

Page thought long and hard and decided to discard positive answer number 8, the banal original — *Draw Safely From The Well* — in favor of the trenchant command . . .

Cast Aside All Doubt

Page was filled with many doubts, and to make sure he wasn't violating the terms of his spiritual universe, he posed a question: "What do you think? Good advice? Someday I'll need it."

He pressed a key on his laptop, and Ming's answer appeared:

CHANGE BRINGS GOOD FORTUNE

Well, then, that's settled. He closed the lid on his laptop, fell into bed without brushing his teeth, and slept for twenty hours.

▼

On the first day of December, Don Bakstrom called an all-hands meeting. "Morning, team. *Shrine of the Spear* is shipping! How great is that, huh?"

Exaggerated sighs of relief escaped from the gathering.

"Yeah, I hear you. Hard work, I know. In movies, sequels don't always do as well as the originals. But in games . . . hah! . . . they usually do better. *Shrine of the Sword* was a big hit, so we've got a lot to look forward to. Congratulations, all of you."

Scattered clapping erupted from the group, led by Hoffman. Bakstrom held up his hands.

"To celebrate, I'm thinking we have ourselves an early Christmas party. Say, Wednesday afternoon. We'll drink eggnog, maybe some mulled wine, nosh on fruitcake — just kidding — and enjoy ourselves, what do you say?"

Murmurs of assent went around the room.

"Okay, then. Get ready to rock and roll, because after that we've got to roll up our sleeves and tackle *Shrine of the Scepter!*"

The team gave out a little cheer. Bakstrom waved and retreated into his office sanctum.

Dazed and made giddy by the sudden lack of work to do, the group dissolved. One by one, team members pulled on their jackets and tip-toed out the door.

All except Page.

"Yo, Jimmy."

Fillmore turned around at the exit. "What's up?"

"My car wouldn't start this morning. Frost in Fairfax. I had to call Uber."

"You want a ride."

"If it's not too much trouble."

"Sure thing. Where do you live?"

"Over in Fairfax."

Fillmore's car was an ancient Jeep Cherokee. Page couldn't readily identify the color of the paint underneath the glazed and peeling clear-coat.

"Hop in, it's my work car. Runs better than it looks."

Traffic was heavy through San Rafael, so Fillmore headed west on Fifth Avenue, dodging the downtown streets. Then, at the edge of the city he vectored into the secluded Sun Valley district.

"Show you something . . ."

He drove slowly along for several blocks, then pulled to the curb and pointed toward a steep hillside.

"This you gotta see."

"See what?"

"Up there . . ."

A staircase ran from the street up through a set of well-kept terraced lawns to an imposing shingle-style house bulging with gables and balconies.

"What am I looking at?" wondered Page.

"That, amigo, is where our beloved CEO Don Bakstrom lives."

Page studied the place. The shingles were gleaming, possibly power-washed within the week. Faux streetlights paralleled the stairs. The globes were already glowing in the wintery twilight. Groundskeepers were bustling through the yard, hard at work trimming small fruit trees, raking leaves, cleaning up gardens planted along the terrace walls.

Page whistled. "We're in California. I'll bet that house cost a million bucks."

Fillmore laughed. "Try three. Three million."

"That's insane."

"That's Don."

They continued onward into San Anselmo on the Miracle Mile.

"Check it out," said Fillmore. "George Lucas lives here. Used to, anyway."

"What? Where?"

"Not sure exactly. Just another citizen. Hey, I'll show you something else . . ."

He steered the Jeep through the Sir Francis Drake Hub onto San

34

Anselmo Avenue and parked beside the town hall.

"Over here."

He led the way into a little park containing bronze life-size statues of Indiana Jones and — *wow!* — Yoda himself, each perched atop a granite boulder. Page almost dropped to his knees in awe.

"Lucas commissioned this," declared Fillmore. "Imagination Park. When the city fathers hemmed and hawed, he bought the property, razed the building that used to be here, and financed the whole thing."

Page fingered a Yoda ear. "Why would he do that?"

"Because this town, this is where *Star Wars* comes from, my man."

▼

On Wednesday in the Brass Knuckles office, there was a Christmas tree, erected and decorated by Hoffman. Plus beer and wine and catered plates of hors-d'oeuvres. The employees were stuffing themselves with nachos and guacamole and little hot dogs and sliders. Their boss and owner was not present, however, when Hoffman inaugurated the event with a toast:

"Here's to the team that built *Shrine of the Spear!*" she enthused. "It's going to be a big hit. You guys are the greatest!"

There was gossip about the possibility of bonuses. Page was hopeful, but Fillmore shook his head.

"Why not?" asked Page, deflated by Fillmore's negativity. "Does Karen know something I don't?"

"We don't actually live together, Ollie. If she does, she didn't tell me."

Half an hour and many glasses of wine later, Bakstrom arrived. He was carrying a large cardboard box.

"Here he is," whispered one of the staffers. "Bonuses for Christmas!"

"Shh!" commanded Hoffman. "Listen up."

Bakstrom took a position in front of his office and clapped his hands for attention.

"Hey, team! Gather round! We've had a tough year — games are always tough, in case you didn't notice — and you guys worked your tails off for Brass Knuckles. Be proud of yourselves, we shipped on schedule!"

He gave a little cough.

"I've been checking the mobile sales charts, and *Shrine of the Spear* is tracking right up there with *Shrine of the Sword.* Looks like we have another big hit coming, folks, and you each deserve a big reward."

Page nudged Fillmore. "Bonuses, what did I tell you," he said.

Bakstrom gestured toward his cardboard box. "This here is the closest thing I could find to Santa's bag."

He reached in and withdrew several smaller boxes, each one containing a Nintendo 3DS portable gaming machine, and handed them out.

"3DS for everyone!" he said. "*Spear* cartridge vouchers included!"

3DS systems were very cool hardware devices, pedigreed, expensive, and well-made, with a huge library of games to play, so Bakstrom's gifts were not spurned. Nevertheless, audible groans were heard from the group. Bakstrom registered the disappointment with a wave of his hand and a sheepish smile.

"Of course, it would be nice to hand out cash bonuses. God knows you deserve them. But, well, I just can't do that. We've burned through a lot of cash bringing *Spear* to market, and we won't see actual revenue until Apple and Google and Nintendo pay us. Maybe next year."

"What did I tell you?" said Fillmore.

Page gave him a sour nod.

▼

The following morning dawned warm and clear for a Fairfax December, and Page's Honda started right up.

On the way into San Rafael he avoided the heavy commute traffic through downtown by retracing the route Fillmore used to drive him home. Halfway through Sun Valley he passed by Bakstrom's impressive mansion. He slowed for another look at the place where his cheapskate penny-pinching boss lived.

"Whoa," he said as he drew abreast of the staircase.

A RE/Max pickup truck was stationed at the curb, and a couple of workmen were busy installing a post with a sign that read:

FOR SALE

"What the fuck?" he groaned, intuitively grasping bad news.

When he got to the Brass Knuckles office in Terra Linda, he hurried inside. His stomach was churning.

Oh my God, his worst fears realized: on the second floor, the studio door was locked. His fellow employees were milling about. Their faces were drawn, their eyes were staring.

He pushed through them to a note taped over the Brass Knuckles logo. It was brief:

Business closed. Direct all correspondence to:

> *Hatfield & Sawyer LLP*
> *1125 Novella Ave., Suite 500*
> *Mountain View CA 94041*

> *Sorry it didn't work out. May the Sword and the Spear be with you.*

> — *Don*

Page looked around for Hoffman. She was standing at the far end of the hall, looking just as bleak as everyone else.

"Karen?"

Hoffman pursed her lips and gave Page a what-do-I-know shrug.

Fillmore was the last to arrive. He read the note and rapped a contemptuous toe against the door.

"Game over, man."

5
00000101

A Christmas card from Mom turned up in Page's mailbox, announcing the approaching holiday season. There was a hand-written message to accompany the standard celebratory greetings:

Dear Ollie —

Gram told us of your adventures out west. Sounds like you found your feet. We're so glad. When you find the time, why don't you write us a note with details?
Much love,

— Mom & Charles

Page rapped the card against his fingertips, reliving unresolved family quarrels. His gloomy reverie was interrupted by a phone call:
"Oliver . . ?"

"Oh hi, Gram. How are you?"

"I'm freezing. I can't go out, there's a foot of snow outside. The wind is howling. The cupboard is bare."

"Unh-huh, call Kroger, they'll deliver. You won't starve."

"So you claim. It's Christmas. When are you coming home?"

"Uh, well, I'm not. Not this year. Still, um, still settling into my job and so forth."

"I miss you."

"Miss you too, Gram."

"You should have taken that job right here in town. Web Cloth."

"Web Weavers."

"You could be living here for nothing. Housing is so expensive out there in California."

Page cast an eye around his tiny room. "Well, you're right about that." He glanced out his window. Some of the trees on the street below still had their leaves. Live oaks, probably. "But — hah! — at least I've got decent weather. It's amazing. Out here snow stays where it belongs, way up in the Sierra Nevada mountains."

"Go ahead, rub it in. How's your job going?"

"Job's great," he lied. "We just shipped our latest game."

"Full of gratuitous violence and gallons of blood, no doubt."

"Come on, Gram, violence yes, blood no. We don't do blood."

"Well, Merry Christmas. Good will towards men, if you remember. I'm sending a care package to tide you over the holidays. Genuine Polish sausage and an apple streusel."

"Uhh, you want to wait on any mail, Gram. I might be moving."

"Moving — ? Where?"

"Up."

▼

The loss of his first and only job, in a far corner of America where he was still a relative stranger, gave Page a wintery chill. The vital notion of conserving cash vaulted to the top of his brain, and he thought it wise to analyze his financial status. Of the promised $45,000 per year at Brass Knuckles, he earned four months worth, and was paid, sadly, for three: $11,250 total. Subtract $3,500 for rent, subtract $1,800 for taxes withheld, another $1,200 for food, $800 to pay off the credit card that bankrolled his trip west, and $500 to fuel his car. That left what in the bank? $3,500. But wait, when he checked his account online, he discovered that the balance was $2,500. Uh-oh, some of those incidentals, the jeans, the T-shirts, that fleece jacket, a pair of running shoes, TV and Wi-Fi — damn — those things added up. He was in trouble. Unless he was very careful, he was going to become a homeless person begging for change on Fourth Street in San Rafael.

Page opened up his laptop and dove into Craigslist.

He struck out searching in Marin County, but found a stock boy job opening at Feldman's Home Improvement Center, twenty-five miles up the Redwood Highway in Petaluma. He thought it might be a good temporary defense against poverty. Back in high school he stocked all the materials for his father's print shop and kept track of the old man's customers with a SQL database he wrote himself. After his father died, he did the same thing for the new owner.

The commute between Petaluma and Fairfax, assuming he could land the job he was looking at, seemed awfully long. What about a place to live? Craigslist also advertised a housemate request from a location in Petaluma's Royal Ranch Estates.

He didn't need to consult his magic chatbot to make the easy decision. The rent was half what he was paying.

"So you're a computer guy. And you want to be a stock boy?"

Page was standing at a counter in the office of Pat Jarman, Feldman's store manager, a beefy fellow in bib overalls and a CAT baseball cap. He was squinting at Page's hastily printed resumé through wire-rimmed glasses.

Page windmilled his arms in nervous jerky circles as he attempted to explain himself.

"My little company folded. I've done this kind of work before. My father ran a plastic fabrication shop in Chicago. He made drinking cups, soap dishes, little green soldiers, spacemen, flowerpots. I did his inventory, moved and stored all the incoming supplies, maintained the machines, shipped the products. When that business all went to China, Dad opened a print shop. Same thing. Then, when Dad got hit on the head with a bale of penny-saver newspapers, I continued on with the new owner."

Jarman looked Page up and down. Not too tall, sandy hair, blue eyes, thin and rangy, nicely dressed. Clean-cut, he concluded, meaning drug-free. In spite of the kid's confident work summary, Jarman detected an untried youth just beneath the surface.

"This is a physical job. You don't look like you've done much heavy lifting."

Page shrugged uncomfortably. "Mostly typing this year, ha ha."

"You're a college boy."

"Is that a problem?"

"Maybe, maybe not. Ever run a forklift?"

Page's shoulders slumped. "No, 'fraid not. I could learn it."

"How about order systems?"

Page straightened up. "You mean inventory? I designed the database Dad used. It worked, even on our old computers, slow as molasses. Bar code reader, everything."

Jarman adjusted his cap. "I dunno, we don't hire many college grads around here, but I guess you'll do."

Page felt a tidal wave of relief flow through his entire body.

"If you don't mind, why are you hiring anyone?"

Jarman snorted. "What time of year is it? Christmas, ever notice? Seasonal shopping — trees, lights, inflatable reindeer. Mini-tractors and power washers on grown men's Santa lists. We're busy." He paused, took a breath, scowled. "And, lo and behold, ICE swept through last week. Quite a few of our employees were undocumented. Who knew?"

▼

Royal Ranch Estates was a large collection of double-wide mobile homes set on land reclaimed from the marshes bordering Petaluma's east side. Although some of them sported cheerful paint on their trim, all of them had seen better days. Rubbish bins, dying motorcycles, surfboards, old washing machines, discarded sofas, and other household detritus spilled out from under the carports. Page's Honda, itself ancient, was among the very nicest cars parked on the pothole-filled street.

His three roommates were a rowdy trio who grated on Page's sensitive and well-educated nerves. Marko worked a shift at McDonalds. Jesus was a janitor at the local hospital. Maybe that's where the drugs came from. Page didn't know and didn't want to know. Angela did some temp work, but couldn't seem to hold a steady job. She alternated sleeping with Marko and Jesus. All three were stoned and/or buzzed most of the time.

After a couple of weeks, Page was frantic to escape.

Luckily, just after Christmas his supervisor approached him with a proposition.

"Where you living, kid?" he asked.

"Royal Ranch."

"You mean Rotten Ranch. That place, whew."

"Yeah, but I'm broke, and it's cheap."

"Got a friend whose tenant just moved to LA. Got a converted garage for rent. Even cheaper."

"Garage?"

"Not what you think. It's all set up with a microwave, fridge, bathroom. Guy travels — he's a trucker — and just wants someone on the property. Asking $250."

The privacy and the price were both right, and starting immediately after New Year's Day, Page moved in.

The winter storm track, which brought heavy rain and fog to December, moved north into Oregon, and blue-sky days prevailed all through January. Page was mesmerized by the wonderful contrast between Northern California and Chicago.

Without realizing it, he was starting to settle in. He bought a hot plate at Target, bought a *Ten Easy Meals* cookbook at Bancroft Books, filled his tiny refrigerator with food, and taught himself to eat at home.

He paid a visit to Pedals For The People, a counter-culture bike shop, where he bought a used mountain bike made out of recycled parts for $50. He started to ride the twenty blocks between his garage and Feldman's on a daily basis, saving on gas and rounding himself into decent physical shape.

▼

Toward the end of January, when the accounts receivable were cleared, Page printed out the holiday sales charts and brought them to his boss.

"Hello, Mr. Jarman — I'm looking at our December results and our building supplies all the way back to last August."

"Oh?"

"How big is our store? Fifty-thousand square feet?"

"Fifty-five," corrected Jarman.

"And we are devoting a couple thousand of those feet to masonry. Bricks, concrete blocks, retaining wall pieces, and pavers. Sixteen kinds of pavers. Plastic, concrete, brick, travertine, square, round, interlocking, you name it. Lots of pavers."

"Your point?" Jarman sensed a challenge to his management style coming. His brow creased.

"We've got four stores, right?" asked Page.

"Unh-huh, four."

"And they all carry pavers."

"We've got a unified inventory system, so yes, they do."

"I know, I checked." Page pointed at the papers in his hand. "Well, guess what? We didn't sell almost any of these things for the last seven months."

"It's seasonal, like everything in construction."

"The Santa Rosa store sold a ton, however."

"Lemme see that shit," growled Jarman. He grabbed the printout and thumbed through the pages.

"What I'm thinking," continued Page, "we only have a few of those John Deere mini-tractors out front. We sold a lot of those things, and made a lot of money on them."

"And .. ?"

"We could drop the pavers, let customers get 'em from Santa

Rosa, and double the square feet we have for tractors, lawn mowers, generators, barbecues."

Jarman stifled an angry retort. He studied his junior employee with something approaching respect.

"Okay, kid. Nice idea. Nice to see you're awake on the job."

"Thank you, Mr. Jarman."

"I doubt we'll follow through, but good thinking."

Page heard his idea being summarily foreclosed. He wasn't ready to give up. "I could move the stock myself, I can handle that forklift."

"I'll think about it. Now — go back to work."

"Yes, sir."

Page was disappointed by Jarman's failure to appreciate his ideas, but was resigned to the dismissal. However, two days later Jarman circled back around to Page, who was slapping bar-coded price tags on a line of wheelbarrows. He presented a cup of hot coffee and took a seat on a wrought iron patio chair.

"Cream and sugar for you, I'm guessing."

"Whoa, thanks," said Page.

"Black for me. I'm old and tough."

Jarman took a sip and leaned forward with a sharp eye on his new employee.

"You're green, but you look like you know what you're doing — most of the time, anyway."

"Um, that's, um, good to hear."

"Don't get your head swelled up. Feldman's? You're just a stock boy at the moment. But there's a career path could open up here. Good prospects are like hen's teeth. I could put you on the management training track, what do you say?"

Page was stunned by the offer. A vision of life spinning away in an unknown direction made him dizzy.

"Geez, Mr. Jarman, that's a great offer."

"Well — ?"

Page took a big swig of coffee. He let the idea swirl through his head, trying to comprehend what accepting would mean.

"I better think. My last job was writing code for a video game. That's what I'm best at — computer software."

"I get it — and that's something you could pursue right here in our company. We rely on software. Apps and such. You could consult, make a valuable contribution."

"I'm not sure . . ."

"Steady job, and the money would be pretty good."

"Wow, that sounds . . . really great."

▼

Page didn't know what to do. A big life choice was looming, and he was sure he would need the emotional support of his chatbot app to help him make a good decision.

Only one problem. He didn't trust the pseudo-random number generator he wrote and was using. Given a starting seed, the numbers, however random looking, always popped out in the exact same sequence. And he wanted, greatly desired, nothing less than the holy grail of *true randomness.*

On the internet he discovered the surprising way the Multi-State Lottery Association's random-number generator worked: the computer involved took a reading from a Geiger counter that measured radioactivity in the surrounding air, specifically radioactive particles randomly popping out of the man-made element Americium-241 in accordance with the laws of quantum mechanics. The emissions happened at unpredictable moments in time and told the lottery computer how to generate a winning number that was truly random. The computer then did so using the same algorithm found in everyday software, something called the Mersenne Twister.

Page did some research and learned that household smoke detectors used Americium-241 to sense fires. He purchased one from Feldman's with his employee discount and set about connecting the radiation sensor to his computer via a USB cable.

But something was wrong with his plan. Bad connections? Bad code? For whatever reason, the concept didn't actually work.

To distract himself, he set out on his bicycle to climb Mount Burdell, a rugged hill fifteen-hundred feet high in the surprisingly open countryside of northern Marin County.

The trail up to the microwave tower was narrow, steep, and gnarly. Inexperience with hard grades and loose dirt meant he had to dismount and push the bike to the next little crest several times.

At the summit he opened a bottle of lemonade and spent a few minutes looking out over the endless carpet of houses and businesses of bustling East Marin. There were no hills like this one anywhere within a hundred and fifty miles of Chicago.

He considered his chatbot. What if he dropped his home-grown pseudo-random number generator and re-coded the app to incorporate the Mersenne Twister instead? What if he called the algorithm repeatedly from the moment Ming appeared on his laptop? Would the uncertain time interval until he actually asked a question produce a true random number? Worth a try, anyway, he thought, pleased with the way the hard climb had settled his mind.

On the way down, he met a rider coming the other way, grinding up the steepest sections without a single mistake. When the rider neared, he observed red hair flowing out of a lime green helmet. It was a young woman, her face half hidden behind a pair of Oakley sunglasses. He couldn't help noticing how her sweat-stained T-shirt was clinging to her breasts. The sight thrilled and embarrassed him. He wanted to wave, but he was determined to ride all the way down without falling, and he didn't dare take a hand off his brakes.

A few minutes later, he was still descending the steep incline as slowly as he had climbed, with his bike's brake pads squeaking against his wheel rims.

"On your left!" came a shout.

The woman he saw riding up was already on her way back down. She whipped past him with a casual salute and zoomed on down the trail, standing on her pedals over the smaller bumps, bouncing into the air on the big ones. He was amazed by her daring speed.

In the evening, back in his garage apartment, he alternated bites of microwaved lasagna with new lines of code to revise his chatbot app. It took him a couple of hours.

Once he was certain that his changes were successfully compiled into the app, he launched it with a tap on his laptop's trackpad. The image of Ming appeared against a black background. Page paused to meditate on the question uppermost in his mind . . . and to wait for what he hoped would be a true random number, delivered from the mysteries of the universe right into his computer. He took a deep breath.

"Should I take the Feldman's job?" he asked.

He pressed a key, and the Master's answer faded into view:

HELP IS NEAR

Page was puzzled by the response. "Come on, Dr. Ming. You can help? So help. I need a real answer." He counted to seven and tapped the trackpad. Ming responded with cool detachment:

A FIRE CLOUDS THOUGHT

"So it's all up to me, is that it?"

He impatiently smacked the spacebar with his thumb and received yet another oracular message:

WILLPOWER PAVES THE PATH

"Well, damn. What to do, what to do?"

With the unpleasant prospect of a career in retail looming, he dismissed the chatbot app and opened his web browser to

Craigslist. There he conducted a grim search for jobs in Bay Area video game development. Anything to counter the Feldman's offer. When the filtered results appeared, he found himself staring at a long list, but when he refined the search to exclude all but locations north of the Golden Gate Bridge, he saw only one possibility:

> *Programmer wanted for multiplayer game.*
> *Familiarity with C-style languages required.*
> *Ability to hit the ground running required.*
> *Salary open to negotiation.*
>
> *Apply:*
>   *Arrowshaft Interactive Media*
>   *Building One*
>   *New Horizons Enterprise Center*
>   *Novato CA 94949*
>   *jobs@arrowtintermed.com*

He re-opened his chatbot.

"Hey, Ming, look at that, will ya! What do you think? Should I apply?"

He waited for a few seconds to let the shroud of randomness settle over his wise counselor. Then, when he imagined that a significant message was emerging from the ether, he pressed a key. Ming seemed to consider the question, then replied:

PUSH UPWARD WITHOUT FEAR

Page jerked out of his chair, flipping his laptop onto the bed. He stood as tall as possible, raised clenched fists above his head, and shouted to the cosmos:

"Yessssssss!"

6
00000110

The only North Bay game developer looking to hire a programmer occupied one of three buildings in the New Horizons Enterprise Center, a business park located in the newly incorporated Bayview District of Novato, Marin County's second largest and most ambitiously growing city. The area comprised a low rise of ground and surrounding marshland about half a mile south of Hamilton Field, a former Air Force base. Aside from an unfinished housing development on Bayview's slopes, the imposing New Horizons complex was the sole taxable occupant of Novato's expanding territory.

Page drove south from Petaluma, exited the freeway on the Hamilton off-ramp, and cautiously followed a maze of unfamiliar streets south and east into grassy lowlands divided by sluggish streams and tidal sloughs.

An impressive sign in raised bronze letters on a concrete pedestal identified the multi-story Arrowshaft offices. Inside, the receptionist directed him to the fourth floor where Vivian Romero, the motherly human resource manager who fielded his online application, met him at the elevator and identified herself. Page registered a comfortably voluminous woman in her fifties, shook an offered hand, and followed her into a brightly lit conference room overlooking San Pablo Bay.

Page hesitated in the doorway. Facing him at one end of a long oak table was a slender man in his thirties whose hair was so blond it looked transparent. On one side a young woman in a frilly blouse was leaning over the table, toying with a coffee cup. Her golden hair was swept up in an elegant chignon. Romero sat herself down opposite the woman, adjusted her dark blue blazer, and invited Page to take an empty seat.

"Mr. Page, I'd like you to meet some members of our team. Vitus Lozoraitis, our lead programmer, Brava Erpenstock, our marketing manager, and me, here for HR.

Page sank into the closest chair and gave the group a shy little wave.

"Why don't we begin by having you tell us what brings you to AIM?" prompted Romero.

Page was confused. "Aim?"

Romero smiled. "A-I-M — shorthand name for our company. The initials?"

"Oh, right, A-I-M." Already, Page felt like an idiot.

"So, you called us. You're a programmer?" asked Lozoraitis in a hopeful tone clouded by obvious doubt and a heavy Baltic accent.

"Yeah, I am," answered Page, once he decoded the question.

"What are you good at?"

"Uhh . . . well, C-style stuff, C# mostly. My last game was a mobile app for iOS, Android, and the Nintendo 3DS."

"Unity?"

"That's right. My specialty."

"We don't use Unity here." Lozoraitis shrugged apologetically. "But maybe we should. Our engine . . ." He trailed off.

Erpenstock pushed her coffee cup away and impatiently tapped a pen on the table. "What company were you with?"

"Brass Knuckles. We shipped *Shrine of the Spear* in December, and whoops — Merry Christmas, everybody — the company went under next day."

Lozoraitis snorted. "Don Bakstrom's outfit, right?"

Page nodded. "Yeah, I guess he owned it."

"That guy. Big asshole, pardon me."

"Yeah, well — that's the polite term."

Lozoraitis stood up and shoved a sheet of paper toward Page. Romero relayed it into the applicant's hands.

"Here's a snippet of C code. What's the output?"

Page studied the printout:

```
#include<stdio.h>
main() {
    char s[]="hello", t[]="hello";
    if(s==t) {
        printf("equal strings");
    }
}
```

Page knew he was looking at a trick question, but it took him a few moments to figure out the puzzle. While he was thinking, he noticed that his interviewers' faces were getting longer and longer. Finally . . .

"Aha. Brackets are empty, no element in either array. Um, there is no output, this function isn't checking the strings, just comparing their base addresses, which cannot be equal, right?"

Lozoraitis nodded appreciatively. "That is correct. Not fooled, good for you."

He passed another sheet along the table:

```
#include<stdio.h>
main() {
    float x = 1.3;
    switch(x) {
        default { printf( "%d", "no case"); }
        case 1 { printf( "%z", "one"); break; }
    }
}
```

Page was so nervous he spent some time staring, even though the code was obviously ridiculous.

"And the output?" queried Lozoraitis.

"Geez, what a mess," said Page. "Switch statements can't use floats, and there is no *percent-z* parameter for *printf.*"

"So — what do you think? Default? Code prints *no case?*"

"It doesn't print anything. It won't compile. If cleaned up, it might print *one*. The default is picked up after all cases, no matter the order inside the switch."

Lozoraitis pointed a finger at Page. "Nice," he said.

At that moment the group was joined by a wiry man with dark eyes, dark curly hair, and an easy manner. He was wearing a black T-shirt and black jeans. Page guessed his age at somewhere above forty.

"Morning, all. This must be Oliver, right?"

Page nodded.

"Oliver Twist, like the Dickens character." He grinned and dropped into a vacant chair.

Page groaned. "Family name on Mom's side."

"Leo Thorpe, glad to meet you. I'm the designer-director guy on our current project. A project — *ahem* — that is way, way behind schedule."

"Software is tough," allowed Page, regretting his comment immediately upon seeing Thorpe's brow furrow into a scowl.

"Right," granted Thorpe. "Looks like we need some heft in the UI department. That so, Vitus? Anyway, you might be the guy. So, questions. If I talk about a *radial pop-up*, what am I referring to?"

Page swallowed. "I think it's kind of a context menu, the kind that keeps all choices the same distance from your mouse or finger."

Thorpe twisted his lips into a smile, acknowledging the correct answer. "And how about *direct manipulation?*"

"Drag and drop."

Thorpe nodded. "Right again. *Anthropomorphic UI?*"

"Touch, I guess."

"Un-huh, good. What about *natural language?*"

"In a user interface context?"

"UI, yes."

"It means voice commands, like *Siri* or *Alexa.*"

Thorpe absorbed Page's responses with satisfaction. "Where'd you go to school, anyway?"

"Camberwell College."

"Never heard of that one. Where on Earth?"

"Chicago."

"Computer science degree, I hope?"

"Not really. They've got a hybrid program called Haptic Design. I took some computer classes, but I'm mostly self-taught."

"Unh-huh, right . . ."

The group fell silent. Page looked down at his shoes. Ms. Romero took up the social slack.

"Any other past employment you'd like to tell us about? Your resumé is pretty brief."

Page paused for a deep breath.

"Back in school, in the summers and on weekends, I handled the inventory for my father's plastic fabrication business, and after he sold it, his print shop. Wrote the databases — SQLite — handled all the purchases, accounts receivable, and so forth."

Romero nodded. She looked around the room at her colleagues. They stared back.

"I see. Well, then, if there are no further questions, I think we have all the information we need. Thanks for stopping by."

Dismissal.

Page cringed, got to his feet, and stumbled out into the hallway.

Brava Erpenstock passed by with a wave on the way back to her desk. "Have a nice day. We'll be in touch if things work out," she called over her shoulder.

Page watched her move away down a long corridor. Now that she was on her feet, he had the full view. To complement her frilly white blouse, she was wearing a short blue skirt with grey stripes that emphasized her hips, black mesh stockings on long legs, and bright red running shoes. Her walk was efficient, purposeful, and also sexy. Just before she turned into an office she reached up, pulled her hair loose, and let it fall over her shoulders.

"I'll steer you out," said Romero coming up behind Page and taking his arm. He nodded absently, dazzled by the feminine vision that just passed by. "What was the lady's name again?"

Romero chuckled. "Brava Erpenstock. She's in charge of our glamour department."

▼

Page was back at Feldman's tagging flowerpots when the call from Arrowshaft came in. He had given up hope after a week, but here was Vivian Romero on his mobile phone.

"Hello, Oliver. I'm sorry to say that we're going another way on the programmer job here at AIM."

Page was prepared for disappointment, but even so, he was crushed by the news. "Hmm . . . too bad for me. Not that I really had my hopes up."

"Now now, don't despair. We were all very impressed by your interview. You seem to know your stuff. But we got lucky, I guess you'd say. A top talent from Electronic Arts wants to work closer to home in Marin. Years of experience, you understand."

"Sure, I get it."

"However, we also noted your background in inventory management."

"Inventory . . ."

"Summers working for your father?"

"Yeah, right, when I was a kid."

"Turns out we have an opening in our shipping department. You'd be a good fit."

Page was unable to muster any enthusiasm.

"What are the chances to move up? I mean, in case you have to fill another programming slot down the line?"

Romero was upbeat. "We publish all our job listings internally. Everyone is eligible to apply, I can promise you that."

Page thought about the proposal while gazing across the greenhouse at a riot of flowers, bushes, and small trees. They were undoubtedly beautiful. But, he thought, somehow ordinary. Just a lot of merchandise to move with clever tags and sales and promotions.

"What would I be shipping?"

"Oh, T-shirts, action figures, coffee cups. Game tie-ins."

"That old story — I'll be swabbing out the elephants, but hey, Ma, I'm joining the circus . . . um, sorry, shipping department."

"Don't be too sorry. We buy goods wholesale, we get orders to sell at retail — with a nice markup — and we fulfill those orders. We call our operation *Fulfillment.*"

7

00000111

Fulfillment.

The AIM warehouse, such as it was, occupied the rear half of the Arrowshaft building's first floor. No wood paneling here, far from the offices of sensitive knowledge workers. No carpeting on the concrete floor. Industrial shelving lined the walls, filled with cartons of fan goods manufactured in various low-wage Asian countries. Stacks of cardboard boxes were tucked under a long bench in the middle of the room. The work surface was equipped with rolls of brown wrapping paper, tape guns, sheets of tissue paper. A cloth bag filled with cornstarch packing popcorn was hanging from the ceiling. A chute to deliver the stuff dangled down over the work area.

Romero gave Page the tour, explaining the operation in general terms. When she arrived at the manager's desk in one corner, she introduced Page to Gary Ozunas, the manager.

"Morning, Gary, here's your new workhorse."

Ozunas nodded, half-elevated himself out of his seat, and gave Page a perfunctory wave.

Romero continued on, leading Page through a forest of boxes to the department's loading dock. There they ran into the other shipping employee, a mousey young woman with grey eyes and straight brown hair chopped into a clumsy pageboy. She was wearing a worn and schmutzy *Legend of Zelda* T-shirt over faded jeans. She paused in her efforts to load fifteen cartons of tacky game memorabilia onto a hand truck.

"Oliver Page, meet Emilee DuFrayne, your new partner in heavy lifting."

DuFrayne removed a pair of work gloves, tucked an unruly strand of hair behind an ear, and offered her hand.

"It's Duffy."

"And I'm Ollie. Nice to meet you."

DuFrayne nodded. "About time we got some muscle around here. You can start by helping me move this pile of crap that just came in."

Romero forced a wan smile.

"Looks like you two have a busy day ahead." She pointed at the ceiling. "Me too . . . upstairs."

She turned and excused herself with a little finger wave.

DuFrayne handed Page a pair of gloves. Together they cleared the loading dock in three trips.

Page removed his gloves and wiped his brow. "That guy Ozunas. What's he doing while we sweat it out?"

"Paperwork, I guess. Something comfy, anyway."

"And that name? Where's he from?"

"No idea. Behind his back everyone calls him *Ozone.*"

"As in *zoned out?*"

"You got it. What a jerk. Butt crack when he bends over. Smokes in the toilet. It's disgusting."

Page decided the mousey look wasn't DuFrayne's whole story.

"Oh boy," he said, being careful not to actually agree.

"Welcome to the Fun House, Ollie."

▼

When Page arrived next morning, Ozunas waved a six-foot long paper tape at him. "Today's list," said Ozunas. Gotta hit UPS by four, so get going."

The tape was actually the shiny backing of a couple of dozen peel-off shipping labels.

Page studied them uncertainly. "I don't see any orders. What am I shipping?"

"See the computer on the counter there?"

"Yeah . . ."

"Orders are all in our Access database. Have at it."

Page stood in front of the computer and stared unhappily at a blank screen. Ozunas followed him and clicked the mouse on a tiny icon in the taskbar. A window popped open.

"Check the labels against open orders, like you see here . . ." he tapped a finger on a checkbox."

"Oh yeah, got it."

Ozunas gave the new hire a calculating look. "How much they paying you, kid?"

The question made Page very uncomfortable.

"I, uhh, thought salary numbers were confidential."

"Mother Romero tell you that?"

"Uhh, yes she did."

"Oh for Christ's sake. Come on, how much . . ?"

Page swallowed, stuck his hands in his pockets. "Well, thirty-seven."

"Thirty-seven thousand . . !?"

Page nodded. A feeling of guilt crept over him.

"Jesus, that's almost as much as I make. That's Arrow-fucking-*shaft* for you!"

He turned back to his desk shaking his head in disbelief.

Page got down to work. After ten minutes, DuFrayne showed up to help. While he read off the orders, she pulled goods from the shelves and took a hand boxing and taping.

"What's the deal with these body parts?" wondered Page, puzzled by the number of requests for little plastic heads, torsos, legs, and backpacks.

DuFrayne shook her head. "Didn't you check us out before your interview?"

"Sort of."

"Well, our current big hit is *Combo Warriors*. Ever play it?"

"Not really."

62

"Me neither. Think of that Lego game, or *Disney Infinity.* All knockoffs of *Skylanders,* right?"

"Activision's toys-meet-video-games."

"Same thing, except in our game the characters have separate parts that you collect to mix-and-match for superpowers."

Page dug through an open box and hauled out a flat disk-like device trailing a USB cable. He held it up for inspection.

"That's our *Fable Factory.* Snap your character's parts together, place it on that pad you're holding, and, voilà, it jumps right into the game on your screen."

DuFrayne reached into the box and pulled out a little red head that featured evil teeth, yellow eyes, and angry black horns.

"That's what we're shipping — game parts. And this little beauty is the most treasured item."

"What is it?"

"The *Dark Devil Head.* Doubles the superpowers on any character."

"Lemme see that thing." He turned it over in his hand. "Do the eyes light up?"

"Of course they do."

"Of course they do," echoed Page, lost in thought. "*Combo Warriors.* A hit. Who knew?"

▼

Later on, Page was checking the Dark Devil supply. He was worried about running out of their most-ordered item. The database claimed seventeen cartons on hand, each containing twenty-four items, but a physical search only turned up sixteen. He took his concerns to DuFrayne. For some odd reason, his usual diffidence around the opposite sex did not extend to his new colleague. Maybe, he thought, it was because she didn't exude the slightest hint of sexuality.

"Hey, Duff, we're missing a bunch of Dark Devil Heads."

"You sure? I didn't notice."

"Yup."

"My advice? Let it slide. No rock leaky boat."

But Page did not let it slide. He was outraged. He never went to mass or confession, but his Catholic upbringing had stayed with him into adulthood, and it sharpened a stern moral streak running through his timid heart. He immediately raised the issue with his boss. Ozunas was cynically indifferent.

"Those fucking Malaysians. What's the damage? One box? This happens all the time. They never ship the full pack, those bastards. Probably selling them on fucking eBay."

This possibility disturbed Page.

"What do you want to do about it?"

"Nothing to do. So our profit margin shrinks some tiny percent, so what? We live with the problem."

Page absorbed the business lesson in silence and slouched back to his workbench. There he glumly adjusted the inventory database to reflect the department's small and apparently insignificant loss.

8

00001000

Page endured a slow-and-go commute south on the Redwood Highway to the Hamilton off-ramp and then a speedier run through back streets to the New Horizons Enterprise Center. The agonizing trip was now routine, but every day he griped inwardly about the lack of alternative routes.

He left his little Honda in a far corner of the Arrowshaft parking garage, hoisted his backpack, and headed for work.

While he was hiking across the concrete expanse, Brava Erpenstock wheeled into the garage in her BMW and slipped into a spot reserved for company officers.

They arrived at the garage elevator together and shared a ride to the first floor. Page wished he had some clever remark at the ready, but he was tongue-tied by the mere presence of the casually gorgeous marketing woman, who, he noticed, wasn't much older than himself.

She gave him a professional smile, indifferent to the effect she was having. "Oliver Page, right? That's your name?"

Page swallowed. He was having trouble with the question, because he was fascinated by Erpenstock's electric blue eyes and by the perfect teeth behind her full lips. Also by her sharp little nose. He thought her nose was especially attractive. Oh, and yes, those perfect round orbs under her blouse, too. "Yeah, um, that's me, Ollie to my friends."

"Well, Ollie, nice to see you joined our team. How are you settling in?"

"Doing okay."

"Good to hear."

They parted in the foyer. Page watched Erpenstock walk across the reception area to the main elevator and press a button. He was riveted by her stride, by her gestures, by her chic clothes. He sighed as the elevator door closed. The young goddess was now ascending into Arrowshaft heaven on the fourth floor.

He tugged at an earlobe. He shook his head to clear his senses. He mumbled her unusual name, "Brava . . ."

He was in love.

In the gritty quotidian reality of the shipping department, his first duty was to accept a new shipment of toys and trinkets out back on the loading dock.

The UPS man handed him the manifest and a receipt. He signed both.

"Morning, Ollie."

Emilee DuFrayne climbed onto the dock. She handed Page a cup of hot coffee and downed a slug of her own.

"Hey, thanks, Duffy."

"So, what have we got?"

"More Dark Devil heads, looks like. And some Dark Devil coffee mugs."

"Whoopee. You count 'em?"

Manifest says twenty cartons — I count twenty. Confirm?"

DuFrayne ran a finger over the boxes. "Twenty it is."

"No cheaters this time. Lucky us."

"Let's be sure." DuFrayne used a box cutter to slice open each box. Twenty-four items in each, as promised.

▼

On the following day, Page recounted the shipment. Only nineteen cartons. One of them was missing.

He looked for Ozunas to report his new discovery, but the Fulfillment boss was not at his desk or anywhere else.

"Let's have a look at Craigslist," said DuFrayne.

Without much effort they turned up three different offerings of *Combo Warriors* items for sale, one targeting the North Bay, another

San Francisco and the peninsula, the third Berkeley and Oakland. The postings were obviously related; they shared a phone number.

"Ozone, you think?" wondered Page.

"No name, but I'm suspicious, for sure."

Page walked around in a circle, thinking hard. He raised a finger. "Idea — we go to the front desk, get the receptionist . . . Sara, right? Get her to call. We listen in, and . . ."

". . . if we hear Ozone's voice, we know," said DuFrayne, finishing the thought.

"Yeah."

The receptionist listened to Page explain his idea, and nodded. "I'll use my own phone, just in case whoever it is might spot the company number. Have a listen, I'm turning on the speaker."

What they all heard was a recorded message advertising rare Dark Devil heads for thirty dollars apiece. Page and DuFrayne were pretty sure the voice belonged to Ozunas.

"What about it, Sara?"

"I don't deal with Mr. Ozunas very often. But I recognize his gravelly voice from when he calls in sick, like today."

▼

"What do we do?" queried Page. He and DuFrayne were sitting on the loading dock, dangling their feet over the edge.

"Do about what?"

"Pardon me? You know what. Our supervisor is a thief."

"That's true," acknowledged DuFrayne. "But here's the thing. I like my job. We report him upstairs, they might shoot the messenger, know what I mean?"

"No, I don't. We've got an obligation."

DuFrayne laughed. "Wow, you never held down a real job before, that's obvious. Corporations? They're funny. You never know how things will fall out."

Page was unconvinced.

"Look, I'm new and maybe whoever runs our department will fire me while I'm still technically on probation. But you've been here a while, yes?"

"Two years."

"So — they'll listen to you. They have to."

DuFrayne shook her head. "You know why I work here? At my old job, my boss was harassing me, and I reported it."

"Sexual harassment?"

"What else? Anyway, management liked that asshole better than me. So guess what? I got canned."

Page took a deep breath. "Well, then, it's up to me."

"Derp! It's your funeral." DuFrayne squinted at the raw recruit and his ridiculous determination. "But if you insist, we're considered part of marketing. Beautiful Brava runs our department."

Page grinned. "Really?"

DuFrayne rolled her eyes to the sky above. "What is it with guys?"

▼

Page pressed a button to summon the Arrowshaft elevator and, once inside, gritted his teeth and firmly pressed another button to command a trip to the fourth floor.

The door opened on a view of a conference room behind frosted glass walls, a corridor lined with glass-fronted offices, and in the other direction, a sea of cloth-covered cubicles whose occupants were heads down at their appointed tasks.

He stuffed his hands in his pockets to quiet his nerves and strolled along the corridor as if he belonged there. Brava Erpenstock was sitting behind a desk in the third office he passed. She was glued to her computer screen, writing emails. He forced himself to breathe normally and knocked.

Erpenstock looked up from her screen. She frowned, evidently having difficulty identifying her visitor. Then recognition dawned, and she motioned him inside.

"Oliver Page," she said. "What's up?"

Page gulped, nearly overwhelmed by Erpenstock's dazzle factor. "Hello, Ms. Erpenstock." He struggled to control his voice, which sounded squeaky in his ears. "I, uhh, I was told you run the shipping department. Downstairs, where I work."

"Yes . . ."

"Well, I'm here to report a theft. Um, probably part of an ongoing series of thefts."

Erpenstock pushed her keyboard away. She picked up a pen and drummed the tip on her desktop.

"What kind of theft?"

"We receive shipments of our little toy *Combo Warriors* heads, bodies, and so on, in twenty carton lots. Yesterday a new shipment came in, just fine, all twenty accounted for, and today a carton of Dark Devil heads, our most important item, is missing."

"Could be misplaced, right? Last time I was down there, boxes everywhere."

"Could be, but we went up on Craigslist and found three different postings to sell those things."

"Craigslist, eBay, our stuff is all over the place."

"Sure, gotta be, huh? *Combo Warriors* is hot. But there was a phone number to call, and we did. We got voicemail. Who left the message? Gary Ozunas."

Erpenstock sat back in her chair. "You've got to be kidding me."

"Sara, our receptionist . . ?"

"I know her."

"She recognized his voice too."

Erpenstock stood up and crossed her arms. She paced back and forth behind her desk. Then she moved to her door and pointed down the corridor.

"Well, Oliver, looks like we've got a problem. A situation, apparently. Glad you noticed. Good work. But now, this is a matter for HR. Viv Romero — her office is right over there."

Page crossed to an identical office on the opposite corridor wall and peered in.

"Ms. Romero?"

"Hello, there. Ollie, right?"

"May I come in?"

Romero gestured to the visitor's chair by her desk. "Have a seat. To what do I owe the pleasure?"

Page sat down, pushed his hands between his knees, and leaned forward. "I've got some bad news, ma'am."

Romero sharpened her focus on Page. "Oh?"

"We've got a theft in the shipping department."

"You've got a theft."

"Missing *Combo Warriors* stock. Stock that's for sale on Craigslist."

Romero sighed. "That's a shame. But it's awful hard to track down petty thieves. Cops don't give a damn."

"No, they've got bigger worries . . . but we know the thief's name."

"What?"

"It's my supervisor. DuFrayne and Sara in reception and me — we heard his voice leaving a phone message."

"Ozone . . ?"

"Yeah, him."

"What's the number? This I gotta hear."

Page rattled off the number, Romero dialed it up, and listened. As the message kicked in, her brows furrowed and her face darkened. After a few seconds, she slammed the phone down.

"I'll be damned."

She tapped some keys on her computer keyboard, calling again via Skype while opening another app to capture the audio stream. This time they both heard Ozunas' voice as Romero recorded his incriminating identity.

"He's a thief all right. And what a dumb ass . . ."

More tapping.

"I've got Ozone's contact info here" — she pivoted the computer monitor to show Page — "and the number you just gave me is listed as his personal mobile number."

"Wow."

Romero's face was red with righteous indignation. "That man! And look!" — she pointed to a data entry on her screen — "we gave him a good performance review not three months ago."

Page immediately felt guilty. "Hope I wasn't talking out of turn. Maybe it's all a mistake."

"Don't be ridiculous. He's fired! As much for being such a moron — my God! — as for stealing our stuff."

"Don't you have to give him like three warnings or something? He's going to be pretty angry when he cleans out his desk."

Romero shook her head. "With conduct like this? Don't worry, I'll handle everything. You will never see him again."

"What about the department? We're jammed, everything's piling up. We need help."

"Sorry, that's a problem for you to solve. We're not hiring. In fact, we're downsizing somewhat."

Romero saw Page's face turn pale.

"All by attrition, you understand. Nobody else is getting fired, especially not you. You're getting a promotion."

"And DuFrayne? She's been here a lot longer than me."

"I like your initiative. Use it on her."

She grinned playfully.

"As of now, *you* — Oliver Page — are AIM's new Fulfillment Manager, with all the rights and privileges pertaining thereto."

"Privileges?"

"That's a joke. There aren't any."

"Where's Ozone?" wondered DuFrayne when Page returned to the shipping department.

"Well, I talked to Ms. Erpenstock about him —"

She winked. "Of course you did."

"She didn't seem to know what to do and sent me over to Ms. Romero in HR, who listened to Ozunas' voice message like we did . . . and fired his ass."

DuFrayne let out a triumphant whoop. Page retreated a step, reflexively avoiding a possible hug.

"That's wonderful!" she burbled. "I gotta say, I was worried, I had my doubts. You did great!"

Page acknowledged the compliment with a shrug. "Thanks. That's not all the news."

"No? Spill!" She smiled, anticipating delicious details.

"They aren't willing to hire a replacement."

"Hah! Ozone never did a lick of work anyway."

"And . . . I got promoted to manager. I'm supposed to start running our department here."

DuFrayne's smile abruptly vanished, obliterated by an animal growl that rose up from her chest and turned into a bellow: "You? The manager? That is so fucking fucked!"

Her hands shot up into the air. Her arms flailed.

"I've been working fingers-to-bone for two fucking years! And you waltz in . . ."

She began stalking back and forth, back and forth, like a metronome. Her face was set in a grim scowl, her complexion was bright red. "You, the new kid in town, sucking up to management!"

Page maneuvered behind the workbench out of arm's reach, just in case. "I asked *you* to report the guy, remember?"

DuFrayne snarled.

"Big raise, right? How much are they paying you?"

"Uhh, no raise. I'll bet you're making more money than me," he offered hopefully.

This stopped DuFrayne in her tracks. "Maybe I am. Maybe not," she grumbled.

Page desperately wanted to defuse the situation. "Here's my deal, what I'm getting —"

DuFrayne shot a hand out toward her theoretical new boss, palm-up. "Stop! I don't want to know. Don't spoil my only consolation, you little dweeb."

9
00001001

Doyle Magowan, Arrowshaft Interactive Media's seasoned Chief Executive Officer, and Benjamin Seabury, AIM's youthful Chief Financial Officer, were huddling in Magowan's corner office, discussing company fortunes and the uncertain mood of their corporate parent, Almaden Capital Management, a private equity firm.

"We've got two days," cautioned Magowan. "Our ducks must line up."

"Combo Warriors was a hit. We're profitable, they can't complain," said Seabury, glancing at a computer printout in his lap.

"On paper, we are. But not big, like Almaden's pharma group, the generic ibuprofen kings."

"That's true. Drugs are a racket."

"So we need to talk around our problems. The new game is going to ship six months late. At best."

"Do we know why?"

"Something about the player's in-game presence, his avatar AI. Christ, I don't know."

"I'll talk to Saint Vitus, get the scoop."

"Yeah, good luck."

The two executives could never seem to grasp the details of software development for much longer than it took to explain them.

"What's our run rate these days?" wondered Magowan.

"We're burning through three hundred thousand dollars a month, looks like."

"Christ Almighty. Three hundred K. Goodbye to our meager profits. Goodbye to our co-op ad buy with Walmart. We'll have to pay a drop fee to the TV networks."

Seabury shifted in his chair. "On the bright side, *Pony Corral* on the 3DS is on time and on budget. We'll sell a million units."

"Jesus, Ben, who cares? Almaden execs are sharpening their knives. This delay could sink us."

Magowan rose from his ergonomic Aeron chair and stood at the window, looking east toward San Pablo Bay. He ran a hand through his wavy dark hair.

"Worse, we don't even have a title."

Seabury was puzzled. "What's wrong with *Combo 2?*"

"Didn't test that well, apparently. Brava thinks our so-called hit would have hit a lot bigger with a better name."

"Let's get Brava in here, get a reality check."

The AIM marketing manager duly appeared before the two men.

"*Combo 2?*" she asked rhetorically. "A boring sequel to Mindy's original boring pick. We can do better."

Magowan flopped back into his chair. He moved papers around on his desk. "That's why Mindy doesn't work here anymore and you do." He picked up a memo. "And your idea is going to be *Skinners?* It's punchy, I'd go for that."

Erpenstock winced. "Sorry, not bad, but it got taken. Some British company. Enviable Media, I think."

"You can't copyright a title," protested Seabury.

"No," admitted Erpenstock, "but they've got a trademark. It's TM-ed. Do you want to duke it out in court?"

"What then?"

Erpenstock removed a tiny battery-powered digital projector from a jacket pocket. She propped it up on a slender tripod, aimed it at the office wall, and flicked a tiny switch. A colorful PowerPoint slide flashed into view with a title proposal done up as a snappy logo.

"How about . . . *Evolvers?*"

Magowan and Seabury looked at each other. Magowan's lip

curled. "Come on, Brava, that sounds like a fucking science lesson."

Erpenstock sat down on a corner of the CEO's desk. "Okay, then, it's got to be — *PieceMakers.*"

"Peace-what?"

She thumbed a button on her projector, and another colorful slide splashed onto the wall with another logo.

"Piece. Makers. Get it? Put together your little avatars, the pieces, and bring peace to the world by shooting every bad guy you can find. What our game is all about anyway, right?"

"Hmm, I dunno. You test it?"

Erpenstock leaned toward Magowan, showing him some cleavage. "We ran a focus group. Trust me on this."

She advanced the PowerPoint presentation to an Excel chart with wiggly lines corroborating her intuition.

Magowan nodded bleakly. "Okay, *PieceMakers* it is."

Seabury nodded appreciation. "Hey, I like it."

Erpenstock smiled. "Thanks, Ben."

Magowan jabbed at an intercom. "Sara? Get Leo the Genius in here." He knitted his fingers together. "We've got to speed this project up."

A few moments later Leo Thorpe stepped into the room.

"Hi-ho, gang. What's the crisis today?"

"Leo, my man," said Magowan. "Brava got us a title for your game."

Thorpe looked around the room. "Want to tell me?"

Erpenstock projected her chosen title on the wall again, and nodded to Magowan, who nodded to Seabury.

"PieceMakers," announced the CFO. "How does it strike you?"

"Cute logo. Lemme think about it. The title is not our biggest problem. We need a new control scheme."

"Our biggest problem, Leo, is shipping this product," insisted

Magowan. "What's wrong with the controls?"

Seabury was equally disturbed, and with considerably more familiarity with the game in question. "I thought putting artificial intelligence into the player's in-game character instead of just the bad guys — combining the spirit guide with the player's avatar — was our main innovation, our big sell."

Thorpe let out a glum sigh. "Everyone hates it. The developers hate it. The testers hate it. We brought in a focus group, and they hated it. Even I hate it, and I thought it up."

Erpenstock pocketed her audio-visual tool. She winked at Seabury. "I've thought about the avatar problem — you can't walk around here without hearing the gripes. So we restrict it to our *Newton* headpiece. It's a special purchase. Problem solved."

Thorpe scratched his head. "Newton? That old Apple failure still stinks."

Who's Newton?" wondered Magowan. "No millennial ever heard of him."

Erpenstock snorted. "Marketing lady rolls eyes."

Thorpe rubbed his nose, thinking things over, then snapped his fingers. "Brava's almost right. Special headpiece. Call it *Einstein* then. Or *Gort*, from that old sci-fi movie."

"Brava, you go, girl," said Seabury.

Erpenstock made a little curtsy.

"Christ, what a mess," growled Magowan. "New controls — how long will I suffer? I don't want to hear two weeks, and I don't want to hear two months."

Thorpe opened the office door and made a signal. After a short delay, AIM's new programmer, the man hired over Oliver Page, shuffled inside to join the group.

"Meet Karsten Vollmer, everybody. He's handling the control rev."

Vollmer waved. Everyone nodded. Erpenstock involuntarily

backed away. The man was short and round and weighed two hundred and fifty pounds. His clothes were dirty, and he smelled.

"So, Kars, how long for our shiny new control scheme?" prompted Thorpe.

"In Real Life? No lies? Three months," said Vollmer in a low voice colored by a faint German accent. "Two if we recruit a decent broheim to validate the UX."

Not what Thorpe expected to hear. He looked like he was about to faint.

Seabury cleared his throat. "Ooh, that will be tough," he said, sucking air through his teeth. "Three months to you means six to me, because I know something you don't — no new hires."

"Then I poach," said Vollmer. "Can I have Lozoraitis?"

"No, he's busy. Admin, *Pony Corral.* It's complicated."

"All right, you want to ship this *dreck* we're building? We use the old control system from *Combo Warriors.*"

Magowan was immensely relieved by Vollmer's sensible fallback notion.. "Duly authorized," he said.

"Except for Einstein," noted Seabury.

▼

The meeting was over, and the Arrowshaft brain trust dispersed. All except Erpenstock, who lingered at Magowan's window.

When she was sure everyone was out of earshot, she turned to confront her boss.

"What about my raise?" she demanded.

"Brava, Brava, Brava . . ."

"I just saved the company, and your ass with it, mister."

"We'll see if you saved us in about six months, if and when we actually ship fucking *PieceMakers.* Maybe then."

"Six months??? You bastard! You *promised* me!"

"I know I did. Can't help it, we're in trouble,"

Erpenstock was furious and she was desperate. Her complaint was half bark, half wail. "This is a *betrayal.* How will I keep my apartment? How will I make the payments on my Beamer?"

>>> 0010

PART TWO

10
00001010

After a couple of weeks on the job, Page discovered a way to relieve the agony of commuting from his garage in Petaluma to the southeast corner of Novato. An online article drew his attention to the Sonoma-Marin Area Rapid Transit District and its recently inaugurated *SMART* train service on the old Northwestern Pacific railroad tracks. It was a short mile from home to the Petaluma Downtown Station, twenty minutes on the rails, and a mile and a half from the Hamilton Station to Arrowshaft. An easy bike ride, and the cost, five-fifty each way, while expensive, was within his means.

On his third day using the train, he wheeled his bicycle into the lead car, lifted the front wheel onto the built-in hook, snugged the back wheel into the lower support bracket, and secured it with the attached lanyard. While he was busy with this task he noticed an adjacent bike with a lime green helmet dangling from the saddle.

As he filed through the cabin hunting for a seat he passed a young woman with flowing red hair buying coffee at the snack bar. Something familiar about her, but he couldn't remember what.

At the Hamilton Station, he was first out the door and away on his bike before the train started to move again. He pedaled along tree-lined streets past a row of converted airplane hangars before veering onto a paved bike path that crossed the old airport runway and led directly to the New Horizons business complex. To avoid the embarrassing workplace consequences of breaking a sweat, he set a moderate pace for himself. He was rolling past fields of dead grass and muddy sloughs, with his mind drifting to logistical problems in the Arrowshaft shipping department, when a shout interrupted his thoughts:

"On your left!"

Another cyclist zoomed past. A woman, evidently. She was wearing a lime green helmet. Red hair was streaming past her shoulders.

He descended into the New Horizons garage just in time to see the red-haired cyclist rack up her bike and enter an elevator connected to Building Two in the business complex.

While he was racking and locking his own bike, he noticed Erpenstock driving into the garage in her Beamer. He casually timed his arrival at the Building One elevator to share another ride with her.

"Um, morning," he said as he stepped into the car.

Erpenstock was staring at something beyond the elevator wall. She ignored him.

"Uhh, any idea what goes on in Building Two?" persisted Page. "I've never been over there."

Erpenstock collected herself and focused on her gawky admirer.

"Oh, morning, Page. Building Two? That's Verifex."

"What do they do?"

"Visual effects. A spinoff from Industrial Light & Magic. That sci-fi film, *Waystation Earth?* They did the alien invasion."

"Cool."

Erpenstock noticed Page's bicycle helmet.

"You ride in today?"

"Yeah. I live in Petaluma."

"SMART train?"

"Unh-huh."

"The company offers discount tickets. Talk to Sara — she'll fix you up."

The doors opened on the Arrowshaft lobby. Now that they were talking, Page racked his brain for any possible way to continue their conversation. "Excuse me, I'm new, as you know, and I was wondering about setting up a bank account."

"Banks, don't get me started . . .."

"Oh no. What should I worry about?'

"I just spent hours on a corporate account. Watch out, banks suck your life away."

With that, Erpenstock strode away toward the company offices, and Page trudged into the shipping department.

▼

What the new Fulfillment manager didn't know was that Erpenstock had just finished the laborious interviews necessary to establish a small company she was starting up.

In her office she wrote a purchase order to obtain the services of High Beam Consulting LLC, and marched into Ben Seabury's office for the CFO's okay.

"Ben, hey, there, I've got an idea," she said.

Seabury smiled, always happy to chat with the beautiful young marketing woman. "Morning, Brava. How can I make your day?"

"With money. Losing our ship date has trashed my advertising plans. We're going to need a lot of help getting *PieceMakers* out there in front of players"

"Assuming it ships."

"Right. Assuming." The mere thought of the catastrophic alternative caused a dark cloud to pass across her face. "If and when it does, I know our ad budget will be minimal."

"Probably. Truth is, almost certainly. What's on your mind?"

"I want to hire a consulting firm, strategize our approach, maximize the value of our limited dollars."

"Who are we talking about?"

"High Beam."

"Never heard of them."

"They specialize in problems like this. They'll develop our publicity, rev up some buzz, slot our ads where they'll be seen."

She waved her P.O. at him.

"Whatcha got there?" Seabury took the requisition and studied it. "Whoa, twenty-five thousand up front?"

"They need a down payment, and ten a month through shipment plus three."

"Lot of dough, babe."

"It's a rounding error in the world of advertising, Ben. Our survival is on the line, isn't that what our brilliant CEO is worried about?"

Seabury let out a sigh.

"Okay, run with it. Get a contract I can sign."

"Thanks, I will. It's our best shot."

Later, over a solitary lunch at Grazella, a fashionable eatery in Novato's Old Town district, Erpenstock ordered a campari and soda and toasted herself.

"Here's to financial security," she said aloud, downing half of her cocktail in one gulp.

When her portabella panini arrived, she ordered a glass of expensive chardonnay and downed that too. Her advertising plan was accepted, and the future looked good.

The future looked especially good because the firm she was hiring, High Beam Consulting LLC, was her very own company, established using her mother's maiden name within the past twenty-four hours, and designed to do nothing more than cash a string of Arrowshaft checks.

"So now I'm a crook," she muttered, finishing her meal with a measure of sweet Moscato d'Asti wine. "So what?"

11

00001011

Page and DuFrayne were hard at work in the shipping department, packing *Pony Corral* action figures for young fans of Arrowshaft's mobile game franchise. Page's mind was swirling with doubts about his itching interest in the department's nominal supervisor, and his doubts forced their way into words.

"Do you think obsessions are dangerous?"

"Are we speaking?' sniffed DuFrayne.

"Yes, we are speaking. We have to. Like, hand me the tape gun, please."

DuFrayne flipped the tape dispenser across the workbench. Page caught it with one hand.

"You're talking about Bouncing Brava, unless zombies ate my brain," she said.

"You noticed."

"Oh my God — noticed! How could I not?"

"So?"

"I see your heart thumping, but she's in another league, boss. Forget about her."

"That's probably a good idea, but I'm having trouble with it."

DuFrayne spread her arms wide and appealed to the ceiling. "Here I am, Lord, working for a child."

She picked up a stack of boxes and shuffled off to the loading dock.

Page watched her move out of sight, then sat down at the department desk, activated his laptop, and opened up his chatbot app. The ancient wizard appeared, eyes staring into his soul.

"Okay, here's my question of the day — "should I, you know, forget about getting better acquainted with Ms. Erpenstock?"

He couldn't bring himself to frame his question more explicitly.

What he really wanted to know was: will she ever go out with me?

Page pressed the laptop's spacebar. The pseudo-random number generator spun its digital wheels, and the home-grown chatbot offered this response:

HEAVY CLOUDS VEIL HEAVEN

"What are you doing?"

DuFrayne was now standing right behind Page, peering over his shoulder at the enigmatic text on his laptop.

He closed the lid.

"Nothing, just fooling around."

DuFrayne pointed a finger at him. "Asking your computer — *Master Ming?* — about your sick fantasies, I'm guessing. That is pathetic."

Page didn't disagree.

"Keep on boxing, Duff, you're doing great."

▼

The object of Page's obsession, Brava Erpenstock, left her office with a *Combo-Warriors*-themed coffee cup in her hand and headed into cube land for a refill in the company kitchenette.

On her way back, the new programmer, Karsten Vollmer, stood up in his cubicle and hailed her with a wave.

"Hey, Erpenstock."

She bristled at the rude tone and shrank back when she realized who was calling her.

"Come here, I've got something to show you."

She gave the doughy man a doughy smile. "Oh, look, I'm really busy . . ."

"No, no, you've got to see this. It's real important."

Erpenstock bit her lip. She threaded her way through the cubicle maze and into Vollmer's tiny space, moving like a princess forced to consort with her poverty-stricken subjects.

"Take a look," he said, pointing at his computer monitor.

On the screen was a window full of text.

"Emails? What's the idea?"

"Notice who wrote them?"

Erpenstock leaned forward for a closer look. The emails were a series of messages between herself and her bank, detailing establishment of the bogus advertising firm, High Beam Consulting LLC.

"The source is your email account," noted Vollmer. "The signature — *Barbara Clifton* — mom's name, maybe?"

Erpenstock turned white, then red.

"Hacker! *How dare you* read other people's emails? That is a clear violation of company policy. You'll be fired for this."

"Really?"

"Absolutely. You are toast."

Vollmer shrugged.

"See, I like to know what's going on in the companies I work for. It gets weird sometimes, and I'm a good detective. High Beam looks suspicious to me. Here's another email from Mr. Seabury, authorizing payments to your phony company."

"Ridiculous!"

"I'm thinking embezzlement. What if I showed this stuff to Ms. Romero or Mr. Magowan? They might thank me for spotting criminal activity."

All color drained from Erpenstock's face. She put a hand on Vollmer's chairback to steady herself.

"All right, you creep, what do you want?"

12
00001100

Doyle Magowan stared at his calendar, contemplating the future of Arrowshaft Interactive Media. He marveled at the astonishing run rate that was bleeding the company coffers. Viewed in some detail, it was worse than he imagined. The more he stared, the more concerned he became. Soon, concerns became worries. He began to sense moisture under his armpits, prompting a call to his Chief Financial Officer.

"Ben, we've got to do something. The Almaden meeting? Naziri, Karnovsky — they have no human warmth. We'll be spitted and roasted like shish kabobs when they hear our sad tale."

"Christ, Doyle, calm down. We've been all over this. We shipped *Combo,* we'll ship *PieceMakers.*"

"You hope. News of the day? Hope is for dopes. I want you to read our people the riot act. Light a fire. If we go down, everyone goes down."

"Okay, okay. I'll get into it."

Seabury let the phone go dead, then made a call to muster the *PieceMakers* leads, Leo Thorpe and Karsten Vollmer, to Arrowshaft's business offices.

"Here's the issue we're facing, gentlemen," said he. "Doyle and I are scheduled to meet with Almaden in the next couple of days. We will be forced to explain our delays and our run rate to men that don't want to hear bad news. They may very well react negatively."

"Negatively?" repeated Thorpe. "Meaning what, exactly?"

"Meaning the end of corporate life as we know it."

Thorpe dropped into a chair.

Seabury pointed at his calendar. "What can I tell them — our owners — about our progress? When do we ship?"

Vollmer bobbed his shaggy head.

"Three months, unless we cut features."

Seabury scowled. "Three months means six months."

Vollmer adopted an ironic grin to acknowledge the scheduling truism. "Probably."

"So cut — cut, cut, cut!"

Thorpe held up a hand. "You realize, Ben, that our game fits into a genre, right? We will be on sale alongside the market leaders in crossover games. Lose features and we lose cred. Reviewers will trash us, and no one will buy a single unit."

"Listen, Leo. Your fucking artistic ideals mean zippity doodah. We need anything to get us out the door while that door is still open. *Comprende?*"

"Re-brand *Combo Warriors,* and call it a new game," suggested Vollmer.

"Sounds like a plan," replied Seabury. "Except for Einstein."

"Yeah, Einstein."

"And the Dark Devil heads. Gotta keep those."

"This is ridiculous," grumbled Thorpe.

"You like your job, Leo? I'm trying to save it. Help me help you. The guy who runs Almaden is Iranian, from Iran. How far is that? No sense of American culture, our kind of give-and-take. I worked for the man — he doesn't know a video game from a pistachio nut. All he knows is the bottom line. So take a long look at your feature list and use your scissors."

13
00001101

At Arrowshaft, as in other large organizations, trouble generated gossip. The recent product changes, unkind rebukes, and financial woes constituted bad news that flowed, like proverbial shit itself, unstoppably downhill. Somehow, a casual word from Thorpe to his lead artist, or possibly an offhand remark from Vollmer to a tester, sparked a metaphoric brushfire, a tornado, an explosion of rumors that blew, mouth to mouth, email to email, throughout the company. Heads bent over computer keyboards in offices and cubicles throughout New Horizons Building One, tapping out prayerful revisions to already inflated resumés.

In less than an hour the fear and confusion reached all the way down from the fourth floor into the shipping department, where naïve Page and cynical DuFrayne braced themselves for the worst.

The young Fulfillment manager thought it prudent to consult his chatbot app for advice. His equally young colleague was willing to watch.

"How shall I phrase it?" he asked.

"Phrase what?" she wondered. She was new to Page's form of encouraging divination.

"I have to ask a question. Should I make it negative or positive?"

"I don't know. This is all such supernatural bullshit."

Page emphatically disagreed. "It's not supernatural, and it's not bullshit."

"Of course not. Science rules."

"Don't laugh. We have conscious minds, right?"

"Some of us, anyway."

"So try this — tell yourself to remember something. Say you're watching *Jeopardy,* and they want the capital of Afghanistan. Bing! Kabul pops into your head, but you couldn't explain how the process works."

"I never watch *Jeopardy* . . ." grouched DuFrayne.

"Proving," continued Page airily, "that we also have an *UN*-conscious mind, a mind that's not very well connected to our conscious thoughts."

"You're a college boy. They make you study this in college?"

"So, when I ask a question and get an ambiguous answer, the way I interpret it — in my gut — emotionally — tells my conscious mind what my unconscious mind is thinking. It unifies my mental life."

DuFrayne gave her crazy boss a lopsided smile. "Why are you working for AIM? You should be teaching psych over at Indian Valley."

The sour barb failed to penetrate. Page stoutly believed in his psychological explanation, but deep down he also believed in the Mystery of Life. Without subscribing to any established religious ideas, he nevertheless imagined that some sort of unseen power might be dispensing the chatbot's enigmatic advice.

"Let's try it," he urged. "How about, "Should we quit Arrowshaft?""

"Whoa, there — too blunt. Way too scary blunt."

"Well then . . . is Arrowshaft doomed?"

"No, no, no."

"Okay. Um, should we be planning for life after Arrowshaft?"

"Better . . . slightly."

Page pressed the spacebar. Master Ming frowned, and his answer rippled into view below his head:

LET MANY THINGS PASS

They looked at each other.

"So no, we shouldn't give up." Page explained. "Does this make you feel better or worse?"

DuFrayne considered her reaction. "Better. Little bit, anyway. Relieved is more like it."

"Relieved — you want to believe."

"It's easier than thinking about unemployment."

"Me too. That means we ride it out."

DuFrayne giggled self-consciously. "What a stupid way to run a life."

▼

Next day, Brava Erpenstock appeared in the shipping department.

"Morning, Ms. Erpenstock. What brings you here? How can I help?" What can I do?" fizzed Page, made giddy by his supervisor's close presence.

"I need you to mail an item for me."

"Sure, anything."

"This . . ." said Erpenstock, holding out a small rubbery action figure of Elastigirl, mother of the Pixar *Incredibles* family, attired in her bright red supersuit.

In the background, DuFrayne folded her arms and quietly observed the transaction.

"Sure thing, Ms. Erpenstock. Where to?"

"I sent an address. It should pop up on your computer."

"Okay. Does it have to go priority, airmail, get there quick?"

"Yes. Quick. Overnight if possible."

Page took the little action figure from Erpenstock's outstretched hand. He was too shy to touch her fingertips in the process.

"Got it. Off it goes. Rely on me."

The shadow of a smile appeared and disappeared on Erpenstock's voluptuous lips. She swept her gaze across the room.

"Looks like you've got everything under control here, Ollie. Good job."

She waved and departed.

DuFrayne watched her go. She could not resist taunting Page. "Oh, Ms. Erpitude. How can I help, you? Oh, what can I do? You sound like a total moron."

Page compressed his lips and shrugged. "I know. I'm a dope."

DuFrayne moved to the department computer and touched a key. A mailing label rolled out of the printer.

"Whoa, boss, What's this?"

She held it up for Page to check:

```
Rote Königin Medien
Postfach 74 89 A3 F0 04 76 9E EB
Hannover 30163
DEUTSCHLAND
```

Page studied the label.

"That P.O. box — it can't be right."

"Call the woman."

He did. He was thrilled to hear Erpenstock's voice purring in his ear, even as she confirmed the strange address.

"She says it's correct," he reported.

They packaged up the little red action figure in bubble wrap, dropped it into a box that was too big, filled the empty space with cornstarch popcorn, sealed the container with wrapping tape, affixed Erpenstock's questionable label, added the correct customs form, and mailed the package to the address specified.

14
00001110

With morning orders duly fulfilled, Page biked three miles to the Vineyards shopping center on Ignacio Boulevard, where he ordered a latte and a turkey wrap for an early lunch at Starbucks.

He was sipping coffee and nibbling his sandwich when a young couple dressed for tennis bounced in, chatting and nudging each other. He glanced at the happy pair, drawn by their affectionate laughter. Yuppies in love. They radiated self-confidence, carefree prosperity, obvious success. Page experienced a surge of resentment, which he mistook for hatred until he realized it was envy. Envy for everything they had, and everything he wanted.

Feeling ugly, he bent over his laptop and hid from his unobtainable desires by coding up a new random number idea.

"Dude, what are you doing here?" came an accusatory voice.

He looked up and was surprised to see Jimmy Fillmore striding toward him.

"Jimmy — how are you? Been a while."

"Explain yourself, bro," said Fillmore.

Page gestured toward a page of text on his computer. "I'm developing a light sensor for my chatbot."

"Your chatbot . . ."

"Gotta keep my code hand hot. Shipping packages deadens the soul."

Fillmore picked up Page's coffee and his turkey wrap and threw them in the trash.

"Christ, Ollie, you're a game developer. You can't be seen in Starbucks."

"What's wrong with Starbucks?"

"My God, you don't even know. I'll bet your bike has gears."

"Twenty-one speeds."

Fillmore closed the lid on Page's laptop and tucked it under an arm.

"Come with me, you pathetic dork."

He led Page out the door, down the mall, and across Ignacio Boulevard to the adjacent Meadowlands shopping center and *The Butterfly Coffee Shoppe.*

The late winter day was unexpectedly warm, and waiting for them under an umbrella on the patio was Karen Hoffman.

"Hi, Ollie," she grinned. "What can I get you?"

"He wants a latte and turkey wrap," said Fillmore.

Hoffman rose and headed for the café. "Be right back."

"Need sugar with that," called out Page just before she disappeared inside.

Fillmore pointed to a metal chair. "So sit. We need to talk."

"What's up, Jim? How did you find me?"

"Arrowshaft. Sara? She confirmed you work there, and that scrawny little chick in shipping told me where you go for lunch."

"It's no secret."

Hoffman returned with three lattes and a sandwich for Page. "They didn't have turkey, so I got you the vegan on pita bread."

She resumed her seat.

"Here's the thing, Ollie," she said. "We're starting a small indie company."

"Just the two of us," added Fillmore.

"We want to build a game, and we want you to join up, help us do it."

"Why me?"

"I liked that little game you were working on at Brass Knuckles," said Fillmore.

"My swarm thing."

"Right. Banged together in Unity. We want to publish on iOS and Android. Unity is the way to go, and you're the go-to Unity

guy. I've got some AR code. Karen will do some really cool art,
and we'll have a *Pokémon GO* of our own."

Page thought about the idea. A design opportunity. Programming possibilities. But time-consuming, and the idea of making any
money was pure fantasy.

"I dunno, guys. I need a steady income."

"Come on, dude. You want to be a programmer. You know it, I
know it. And you're shipping fucking coffee mugs instead."

Page squirmed in his chair. He drank up his latte and smacked
the paper cup down on the table.

"Lemme think about it."

Page returned to Arrowshaft with a Windy City Handheld LED
Light Up *Galaxy Spinner* with Flashing LED Lights. He would have
preferred an LED-equipped *Fidget Spinner,* but Target, the only
store within lunch hour bike-riding range, was sold out.

One corner of the Arrowshaft shipping department doubled as a
repair bay, and one of the tools on hand was a soldering iron. Page
spent a few minutes soldering his mail-order light sensor to a USB
cable. When the joint was cool enough to touch, he carefully
wrapped it in electrical tape.

At the departmental desk, he opened up his laptop and spent the
better part of an hour completing the chatbot code revisions he was
working on at Starbucks. He then plugged the USB cable into the
computer and aimed the sensor here and there, assuring himself
that his app actually recorded changing light levels.

Now he was ready to ask Ming to advise on another of life's in-
finite riddles, but just then DuFrayne appeared in the shop.

"Hey, Ollie."

"Hey."

She strolled up to the desk for a good look at Page's laptop.

"What now?" she wondered.

Page let out an exasperated sigh. "Working on my chatbot, if you want to know."

"Don't let me stop you." She picked up the Galaxy Spinner and gave it a whirl. "Toys . . . who are you, one of Peter Pan's lost boys?"

"Give me that," snapped Page. "It's part of my random number generator."

"Oh wow."

"If you're going to hang around, no remarks. This is serious."

"Sorry. By the way, notice anything?"

Page turned around in his chair. "Your T-shirt. *Zelda* goddess *Din* over the *Triforce* logo. That's new."

"Yeah."

Page turned back to his chatbot, activated the spinner, and held his do-it-yourself sensor up to the flashing lights. He was about to inquire about Fillmore's proposal, but then hesitated. He lowered the spinner and took another look at DuFrayne.

"Your hair. You did something to it."

Indeed, DuFrayne's hair was now shorter and nicely shaped around her head.

"I did. Look okay?"

"I guess. I mean, sure. And wait a minute — you're wearing lip-stick."

"The hair lady's idea. Goes with the cut."

"Jesus, Duffy."

"The new me, huh?"

Page was unsettled by the changes in DuFrayne's appearance, vaguely aware that her newfound interest in personal grooming might be meant to attract his attention, a daunting thought.

"Uhh . . . want to see what else is new? I figured out a way to improve the random numbers my guy Ming uses. See, when I spin this Galaxy thing, the lights activate my sensor here, and the color order gives me a real good random seed."

DuFrayne's lighthearted mood abruptly darkened. "Oh, really good, I'm sure."

"I'm going to ask a question, don't laugh."

"Knock yourself out."

She turned away and busied herself in a far corner of the department, counting boxes.

Page flashed the Galaxy Spinner's lights at his sensor again. He closed his eyes and inhaled.

"Okay, here goes — should I help Jimmy and Karen build an indie game?"

He counted off ten seconds, then pressed a key and opened his eyes to the wizard's answer:

HESITATION BRINGS REMORSE

Page closed his laptop and called Hoffman, whose mobile number was still in his contact list from Brass Knuckles days.

"Karen? Indie game? I'm in."

FULFILLMENT

15
00001111

The day of reckoning dreaded by both Doyle Magowan and Ben Seabury arrived. To prepare, the Arrowshaft officers gathered their papers and rehearsed their stories. When they had all the positive points and carefully disguised excuses at their fingertips, Magowan drove them into San Francisco in his fully charged Tesla Model S sedan.

"We shouldn't be worried," insisted Seabury. "We both worked there before Almaden bought Arrowshaft. The company was a basket case until we showed up. And we turned *Combo* into a big hit."

"I'm not worried," said Magowan. "I'm resigned. We are going to be flogged."

Magowan parked in the garage under forty-five stories of the slab-like building that was One Embarcadero Center. They took the express elevator to the twentieth floor, and were shown into an ultra-contemporary conference room with panoramic windows looking out on the Golden Gate and across the bay toward Berkeley and the new Bay Bridge.

They stared at boats coming and going for almost ten minutes, drinking bottled water supplied by the courteous receptionist, before two older men in expensive suits joined them.

"Welcome, gentlemen," boomed the first one, Maksim Karnovsky, a silver-haired man whose round face was deeply tanned. His barrel chest gave his voice an authoritative resonance that made the Arrowshaft executives feel small. He took each of their hands in his, pumped them, thumped their backs, and gestured toward the chairs arranged around the polished birch conference table.

"Good to see you both. You look good. Sit, sit. We talk." Karnovsky was a Russian oligarch who somehow managed to transport his oil money out of the Federation and invest it in

Almaden Capital Management without incurring the wrath of Vladimir Putin or any of the Russian president's corrupt ministers. This feat gave Karnovsky a legendary reputation among his colleagues.

"I would like you to meet my close associate and counselor, Albert Weisbrod. He oversees all our subsidiaries. He looks like owl, with big eyes, *da?* And he sniffs, like Siberian wolf."

"Ha ha, Max," chuckled Weisbrod. "More like a bloodhound. Smaller teeth."

Seabury's palms started to sweat.

"Nice to meet you."

Weisbrod opened a notebook bound in leather and reviewed a fiscal statement.

"I see a delay in shipping your new game. Three months. Loss of co-op advertising opportunities. Cost overrun of one-million-five."

He looked up at the Arrowshaft officers and fixed them with a sharp-eyed glare. "Sound about right?"

Magowan swallowed hard and nodded silently. He didn't trust his voice.

"Well, that is certainly disappointing. Such a delay will wipe out the profit you realized so spectacularly with your last outing. What was the name?"

"Combo Warriors," noted Seabury.

"Ah yes."

Magowan pressed his hands together. He cleared his throat. *"PieceMakers,* the sequel, is assured of success, no matter when it ships, and it will certainly arrive in the marketplace by Christmas."

"How assured?" growled Karnovsky.

"Well, hits breed hits. The game business. *Skylanders* — you've heard of that? Huge. We share the genre. True, discovery is always a big problem — but we achieved that with *Combo,* and players already anticipate *PieceMakers.* They'll be lining up."

"Even without advertisements?"

"Our marketing department has a plan to maximize the impact of our limited dollars. We've hired a consultant, no problem there."

"We are doubtful," said Karnovsky.

"Oh, and our mobile game series is also very successful," chimed Seabury nervously. *"Pony Corral,* our latest, is solid. It will ship on time and on budget."

"Amusement for children," said Karnovsky dismissively.

Magowan gave his CFO a withering stare.

Karnovsky leaned forward in his chair. "Listen to me, gentlemen. Both of you have been employed here at Almaden Capital Management as accountants, so you know how we work, our performance standards. I will tell you the message delivered to me by Mr. Nazari, what he wants you to hear."

Magowan and Seabury bobbed their heads.

"So, it is this way. You must recover your losses from this project, what is it called?"

Weisbrod spoke up. *"PieceMakers,* Max."

"Ahh. This piece of shit you are making will cost your jobs if you lose any more of our money."

Magowan and Seabury exchanged guilty glances.

"You understand? Mr. Nazari would tell you himself, but he is in Hawaii today. More losses, you are dead."

"We have a plan," squeaked Magowan. "We'll dig ourselves out of the hole, don't worry."

"What plan? I am very worried."

Magowan waved his arms. "We're still adjusting, formulating. Let us get back to you."

"Get back to Mr. Weisbrod. I want to hear this plan from him." He stood up and straightened his tie. "That is all, I think. What do you say, Alyosha?"

Weisbrod stood up in turn.

"Good luck, men."

▼

In Magowan's Tesla on the way back to Marin, the Arrowshaft managers discussed their position.

"God in Heaven, Doyle. Plan? We have a *plan?*" Seabury was incredulous. "Are you nuts? We don't have a plan."

"Oh yes we do. We plan to come up with something. It's either that or give up."

"We'll cut features, work everyone night and day. We don't need any bogus plan."

"Yo, Ben? Wake up and smell the skunk. We told them we're delayed three months."

"Yeah, right, that's our understanding of how we're going forward."

"But we both know that three months is six months. A million-five loss is really three million. Unless Brava can get us a world-record pre-order, we are hosed."

Seabury sank down in the passenger seat. "Jesus, we've got our monthly all-hands coming up. What are we going to tell the troops?"

▼

"Good news, folks," declared Magowan in front of all the AIM employees later in the afternoon. "We've just come from a meeting with our owners, Almaden Capital, and they are being very supportive of our current production difficulties."

Sighs of relief ran through the assembly, followed by cynical mutterings.

"Of course we have to perform, and while we are doing everything possible to cut development time on *PieceMakers,* we are also investigating new sources of revenue."

"What new revenue, Mr. Magowan?" shouted one of the artists.

Seabury stepped forward. "We're considering a number of new areas for relatively simple apps. We've got some concepts in mind, and we're soliciting suggestions from one and all — to tap into the incredible talent of our employees. Want to share a thought? Come see me in my office."

After the mass meeting broke up, the two senior executives briefed their immediate reports.

"So, what's going on, Doyle?" demanded Vivian Romero. "Don't lie to me."

Magowan shrugged a guilty shrug. "We've got long-term profit potential in *PieceMakers,* and that's no lie."

Brava Erpenstock's beautiful lips curled into acid doubt. "And . . ? There's a punchline I haven't heard yet."

Seabury touched her arm with reassuring tenderness (or sexist ignorance, depending on one's point of view). "We are being squeezed, Brava, by men with little understanding of game development complexities."

"Now you tell us."

"Right, and we're looking to you for a terrific pre-order. Some evidence to back up our confidence in *PieceMakers'* revenue potential. Show Almaden we've got a winner coming."

Erpenstock scowled. "Sure, if we ever ship."

16
00010000

After the all-hands meeting, Erpenstock and Romero walked back along the fourth-floor corridor together, trudging toward their daily grind. They were companions in anxiety, silently sharing thoughts of a threat they hesitated to name or acknowledge. In the HR office, Romero dropped into her chair with a weary sigh. Erpenstock sat herself down on a corner of the desk. The HR manager reached into a drawer, removed a bottle of reposado tequila, and poured generous amounts into plastic cups.

"Salud," said Romero, handing a cup to Erpenstock.

They clicked plastic rims to signify an alliance against the ugly specter of financial chaos.

"How bad is it, you think?"

Romero knocked back a slug of liquor. She wiped her lips. "This is trouble, no doubt. But I've got confidence in Doyle. He's creative, does well under the gun."

"Wow, you're a lot more hopeful than me."

Romero winked. "I know him better than you do."

Erpenstock almost choked on her drink. She examined the matronly HR woman for any sign of sexual allure and found none.

"You and Magowan? He's a married man."

Romero giggled. "Divorced, honey." She swiveled back and forth to exhibit her current shapeless bulk. "Improbable, I grant you. But it all happened years ago at another company . . . when I was a little bit sleeker."

"Work on your resumé, Viv. That's what I'm going to do."

"Get us some pre-orders, and maybe I won't need one."

"That's a happy thought. I'll be doing my best."

▼

In separate offices down the hall, Magowan and Seabury were both on the phone to management recruiters, alerting them to the vicissitudes of corporate life.

Magowan's chosen lifeline was Soft Touch Executive Placement, a specialist in moving senior executives into new positions.

"EA, Activision — they're okay, but I think a sideways move into venture capital might be the ticket I'd like to punch," declared Magowan.

Pause.

"Oh, of course this is all hypothetical, I still have confidence in our operation right here at Arrowshaft."

Pause.

"Most important, Daisy, if you get a call from Ben Seabury, don't mention our conversation, okay? *Top Secret* isn't a strong enough term."

Seabury's own ideas ran in a different direction, to Northwest Premier Placement.

"Yes, that's right. Vancouver is a possibility, if you can get the Canadians to issue a work permit."

Pause.

"I understand, it's tricky. And frankly, I'd prefer Seattle."

Pause.

"Portland? Shoe companies? Not a chance, no way. Forget it."

▼

Down in Fulfillment, Page and DuFrayne knew little of the fundamental troubles eroding the company, but they did have another mailing label to puzzle over:

```
Rote Königin Medien
Postfach 27 18 62 13 7A 26 D5 68
Hannover 30165
DEUTSCHLAND
```

>>> 0011
PART THREE

112

17
00010001

During the middle years of the Cold War the United States National Security Agency, a nest of electronic spies, expanded rapidly and exponentially. When operations overflowed headquarters at Fort Meade, administrators began leasing offices in the Airport Square Technology Park, ten miles north in Linthicum, Maryland, adjacent to the Baltimore Washington International Airport. The growing facility was named Friendship Annex after what was then called Friendship Airport.

By the second decade of the twenty-first century, following the terrible 9/11 attack, twelve-thousand people worked in several commercial structures on the site, secretly auditing terrorist communication traffic and decoding the plans of anyone who might do the country harm.

On the third floor of building FANEX I, in a far corner of an unattractive cube farm, Warren Ash, a muscular GGE-10-ranked intelligence analyst in his mid-thirties, was studying a computer terminal with dozens of internet connections on display. Three columns of glowing rectangles, each representing an originating device and its target, were marching up his screen in a slow parade.

Ash's job was to uncover unwarranted intrusions into West Coast banks and hospitals and local governments and power plants on behalf of the *Infrastructure Integrity Initiative,* a subdivision of the NSA's Central Security Service.

Today, as on most days, his eyes were ready to glaze over with boredom, but he was a solid professional who knew how to stay alert under any circumstances.

Suddenly, just before the noon hour, one of Ash's little tags glowed red. His sleepy eyes widened. From an internet IP address near Hannover, Germany, someone was jiggling the locks on

Almaden Capital Management's accounts with the Dutch financial firm, Rabobank.

Ash's first reaction was to perform a search inquiry and check on Almaden Capital Management, an obscure Bay Area company he had never heard of. In less than a second he discovered that the company was an investment vehicle with several billion dollars of private money innocently committed to a number of equally obscure endeavors, including a video game outfit called Arrowshaft Interactive Media. His initial interest quickly faded.

Ten minutes later it all happened again, this time from a different Hannover address. His interest ratcheted back up a notch.

Half an hour after that, his NSA software detected three more penetration attempts, all from devices in Germany. He tapped a button on his screen.

"Hey, Sandy, got a bogey on Air Traffic Control, want to have a look?"

Air Traffic Control was the term everyone in the Triple-I section used for the complex software package that monitored infrastructure transactions for the federal government.

Alexander Ufford, a tall and slender GGE-13 in his fifties, set out from his open-walled office alcove and hiked down three aisles and across two more to reach Ash's work station.

"Let me see that," he said, pointing at the screen. He was chewing bubble gum because he was an unreformed smoker, and smoking was forbidden inside the building.

Ash brought up the alert information in a detailed format.

"Here's the thing. I'm looking at an attack originating in Germany, and I also see encrypted traffic running back and forth from our attacker and an IP address in the California Bay Area. That's Almaden's HQ, and also the location of its video game subsidiary . . . what do they call it?" — he snapped his fingers — "Arrowshaft Interactive."

Ufford blew a bubble. "And the point . . ?"

"Connection?"

"Hard to tell. Doesn't look like they have their SWIFT codes set up right, and no password. That's why these attacks are just probes."

"Could be serious, boss. Maybe the attackers want to drain Almaden's accounts. Or — uh-oh — maybe they want to use Almaden to worm their way into Rabobank itself. Maybe bankroll a nest of non-state actors."

"You mean terrorists."

"Can't ignore the possibility."

Ufford stuck his hands in his pockets. "Men on the field, us in the grandstands. What a game."

Ash registered the ho-hum response. "Not excited, I take it."

Ufford shrugged. "What would excite me, what excites Triple-I, is a state-sponsored intrusion. From Hannover? Come on, this looks criminal. A job for Interpol."

Ash's own enthusiasm vanished.

"Okay, I'll backburner the chirps. Now then, the more important question of the moment is, are we touring this weekend?"

"Atlantic City. Five Minis lined up. It will be a parade."

Ash and Ufford were golfing buddies, and they were also auto enthusiasts. Ash had long admired the older man's 1966 Austin Mini Cooper, the tiny collectible Mark I version, and in what began as a sycophantic gesture to his boss, eventually bought one himself. Now he drove it everywhere. Ufford's Mini was equipped with the (relatively) big racing engine. Ash's featured right-hand drive.

Ufford thoughtfully chewed his gum. He blew another bubble and tapped Ash's screen.

"Tell you what — send the encrypted traffic to the Mouse King, get an estimate, and let's see what the Nutcracker comes up with."

"Will do."

18
00010010

At the lunch hour in California, Page was prowling the grounds of the New Horizons Enterprise Center, pointing the camera on his laptop at flowers, trees, benches, signs, and the pale blue sky. He was completely absorbed in the results, which were displayed as long numbers in a little computer program he had written, and he failed to spot a young red-haired woman who was also pacing the grounds, entranced by something she was watching on her smartphone.

They bumped into each other.

"Oh shit, sorry," mumbled Page.

"My fault," said the woman. She took a backward step to observe Page's antics. "What are you doing?"

Page showed her the laptop screen and pointed at it. "The camera looks at things, and I extract colors as numbers to flavor the seed of my random number generator."

The woman had no idea what he was talking about.

"You work at Arrowshaft," she concluded, the only possible explanation for Page's evident weirdness.

"Yeah. I'm upgrading my chatbot. What about you?"

"Trying to catch Pikachu."

"Oh, *Pokémon GO.* Augmented reality. I get it. Got to be one around here somewhere."

"I saw one yesterday, but now . . ."

"Look, I've played that damn game for hours. I've probably got four Pikachus. Also a Raichu. We could trade."

The red-haired woman regarded Page doubtfully.

"No thanks, I will do this on my own."

Now that she was staring at him, he remembered where he had previously seen her.

"You're the bike woman. Your hair. Green helmet. I saw you up on Mount Burdell. You're on SMART every day."

The woman gave him a crisp little nod. "That's me," she said, and turned away.

Page watched her head off toward the Verifex building.

"Whoa, you ride fast," he called out.

She answered without turning around.

"Gotta train. Century coming up."

19
00010011

The callery pear trees lining the parking lot of the Meadowlands shopping center were blooming, and their dark branches were invisible underneath glorious clouds of white blossoms. Spring in Marin County was well underway, and neither an early morning shower, the day's continuing drizzle, nor the threat of a more serious evening storm dulled the spectacular effect.

Karen Hoffman and Jimmy Fillmore were holding down a booth near a gas fireplace in the *Puerto Seguro Mexican Café,* a few stores down from the Butterfly, when Page joined them.

"Hi, guys. Wow, weather. Too wet for biking, I had to drive."

"We ordered already," said Hoffman. "Try the chile rellenos, they are excellent here."

Page shook the raindrops off his jacket, sat, and ordered. Fillmore opened his laptop and started up an unfinished version of the game the three of them were working on.

"Watch this. I pan around, and look, augmented reality! The little monsters are coming for us right here, right across the floor."

They were staring at little squares with googly eyes and wiggly antennas, all marching toward them in between the tables and chairs of the restaurant. Page was impressed.

"Those look like my swarm monsters, all right — boy are they crude — but the AR code, that's awesome."

Fillmore grinned. "I stole it from Brass Knuckles."

"No way."

"Why not? I wrote it, and that place is as dead as a dookie."

Page squirmed in his seat. The idea of thievery disturbed his soul, untested by any of life's important compromises. "Geez, Jimmy, what if Bakstrom finds out? He could sue us."

Hoffman held up a hand for a time out and turned her own laptop around so Page could see the screen. "Look, Ollie — first pass on monsters. What do you think?"

Page studied the collection of little sprite designs, all variation on insect-like critters.

"We're going to be eaten by bugs."

"No? What's wrong with bugs?"

"Nothing. They're fine."

"Okay then," continued Hoffman. "Looks like we've got two big questions to answer — can we finish, and can we sell?"

Page's food arrived, along with a bottle of beer. He stared at the stuffed peppers, then braved a bite. A slug of beer canceled any doubts. "I'm still new to all this Mexican stuff. But . . . not bad."

He opened his chatbot app.

"Let's ask a wizard I know to rule on the big questions."

He aimed the laptop camera at the blue ceiling, then at Hoffman, then at his food.

"Okay, we're ready. Question One — will we ever get to finish this project?"

Before Page could press a key to elicit Ming's advice, Fillmore grabbed his arm.

"What is that thing? Jesus, you're tying our game to a kid's toy?"

"It's not a toy."

"No? It ain't quantum mechanics."

Page looked hurt. "Ever wonder where true random numbers come from? Derp! Try quantum mechanics."

Hoffman intervened again. "Ask already. Throw the dice."

Page nodded a thank you toward the artist and waved at the aged character on his screen. "So again, my question to Ming is — can we finish this project?"

He silently counted to five and pressed a key. Ming blinked.

A STEADY WIND FILLS SAILS

"Okay, we've got his answer. Now, how does it strike you? Agree? Disagree? Our gut reaction, that's what's important."

"Yeah, we can get there," groused Fillmore.

"Right," said Page. "And now, Ming, old thing . . . Question Two— will it sell?"

"Let me do this one," said Hoffman. She pressed the spacebar. Ming blinked again, and his answer followed:

TREAD NOT UNTRIED PATHS

"Uh-oh. Trouble," said Page. "The discovery problem."

Fillmore reached out and closed the lid of Page's machine.

"Forget that janky app. I have some ideas. We will get discovered, and people will line up to buy our game."

Page finished his chile rellenos, finished his beer.

"If you say so, Jimmy."

He looked out the window at a darkening sky.

"I gotta go. Think of a title, guys. Without one, marketing heroics won't do us any good."

20
00010100

Under a palpable cloud of professional doubt, the CEO and CFO of Arrowshaft Interactive Media struggled to rescue their company from the wrath of the owners.

Ben Seabury was near despair.

"It's twenty miles into The City. Karnovsky, Nazari, Weisbrod, those assholes might as well be on the moon for all they know about software development."

"No whining, Ben. We told them we had a plan."

"Yeah . . . 'Adjusting,' you said. 'Formulating,' you said. Some plan."

Doyle Magowan stood up from his desk and moved to the window. He squinted at the morning sunlight reflected off the waters of San Pablo Bay. His mind was whirling, but he could not get traction on any of ten absurd ideas he was entertaining.

"Don't jump, Doyle," said Seabury.

Magowan turned around to face his associate. His expression was pinched by nagging anxiety. He knotted his fists, then unknotted them. The grimace gave way to a wry smile. He seemed to relax. "You know what I've always wanted to do?"

"Not a clue."

"Sail the bay. Get in a boat . . . it doesn't have to be a big one . . . hoist the sail, pull in the main sheet, and just sail away."

"Well, boss, if we don't climb out of the pit we dug, you'll get your chance."

"That's what I'm afraid of. Where's Thorpe? He said he had something for us."

A few moments later a knock on the door signaled Leo Thorpe's arrival. He was carrying a tray filled with Danish pastries, cinnamon rolls, and tall lattes.

"Yo, gents, worry is exhausting," he chortled, handing off the snacks. "You need a lot of sugar to stay on your toes, stay focused on my brilliant idea."

Magowan groaned. "Whatcha got, Leo, besides the snacks?"

Thorpe dragged a chair out of the corner and plunked himself down. There was a pause while he consumed one of the pastries.

"It's really Karsten's idea, but I know how to give it form, flesh it out, make it work."

"Do tell," grumbled Seabury.

Thorpe licked his sticky fingers.

"We will build a simple financial app. People will download it and pay all their bills, deposit money, withdraw money, check their balance, credit, etc., etc., and so on."

Magowan, who was initially hopeful that the company's lead designer would save them, was annoyed. He let out a long sigh. "Good Christ, Leo, there are twenty apps like that. Every bank has one." He raised his smartphone and shook it. "I've got three right here."

Thorpe dug into a cinnamon roll. "Guess what, Doyle? Those apps are all made by the same company, and then superficially rebranded for retail. We will use the same engine for the transaction stuff, so there's very little software development on our part."

"Okay . . . how do we shoulder ourselves into the marketplace?"

Thorpe grinned. "By using the assets in *PieceMakers.*"

"Better explain, because I'm about to call security and have you detained for a psych exam."

"Using our app, people will stroll down a virtual three-dimensional street, where all their creditors have virtual offices, and pay their bills by walking up to a virtual counter. They'll deposit checks by ambling over to their bank, and do so in person — virtually, of course."

"Are you serious?" Seabury wasn't buying.

Thorpe's turn to show signs of irritation. "Not serious. That's the whole point, Ben. The current apps banks use are *boring*. People can hardly stay awake while they stumble through badly designed pages and jab at useless buttons. We're going to clear the decks and make finance *fun.*"

Magowan raised a hand to object. He started a scornful sentence, but didn't complete it. His hand dropped to his side.

'Don't make me laugh," said Seabury, undeterred. "Cruel joke intended."

Magowan took a turn around the room.

"I like it," he declared with a sudden burst of enthusiasm.

"Come on, Doyle, it's ridiculous."

"Maybe ... probably ... who cares? We can sell this to Weisbrod, buy time. Then we use the old code from *Combo* — plus that financial engine, Leo — and we shift the company toward financial services."

"Best of all," interjected Thorpe, "we can still finish *PieceMakers.*"

"Hallelujah," said Seabury, "we're saved."

Magowan was irked by his CFO's obtuse resistance to the concept. "Listen to me, Ben — our clueless masters at Almaden, remember them? They have contempt for our games, but what do they care about? Know about? Think about? Yell about? *Money!* And nothing else. They will love this!"

21
00010101

Page was eating a lonely lunch on a stool in the shipping department repair bay, hunched over the workbench with a soldering gun in hand. He was making another attempt to incorporate radioactivity into his random number generator.

In pursuit of his goal he had stripped the tiny circuit board out of a First Alert ionizing smoke alarm and, following directions he found online, was carefully connecting the sensor output to a USB cable.

When the solder joints cooled, he covered them with Gorilla Glue, plugged the cable into his laptop, and fired up his chatbot.

Master Ming faded into view uttering a skeptical humming sound. Page was pleased to see the results of the audio file he incorporated into his latest code revisions, convinced that the old man had finally come to life.

DuFrayne returned from her own equally lonely lunch and ambled over to watch.

"Still working on your brain machine, I see," she said.

Page slid off his stool. He was disturbed by DuFrayne's undisguised scorn, but didn't quite know how to respond.

"Brain machine?"

"Like you told me, connect the unconscious to the conscious. Am I getting this straight?"

"It's okay to mock me. I'm aware of being weird."

"Weird is the source of your charm." She picked up the smoke detector's plastic shell. "So, what's with the smoke alarm?"

"Consciousness is flammable."

"Hey."

"All right, radioactive emissions happen in spurts. So I made a little Geiger counter. It's my latest way of generating a truly random number."

"You're kidding."

"That's how some of the big national lotteries work, believe it or not. Count the number of emissions in a given time period — even just a few milliseconds — and each time it's completely different. Now you've got a truly random starting seed."

DuFrayne held the tiny circuit board up between thumb and forefinger and examined it closely. "I don't see anything," she said. "This is radioactive?"

"That little foil button in there? Americium-241."

DuFrayne dropped the circuit board on the workbench and took a backward step.

"Don't worry," said Page with a reassuring smile, "Americium emits alpha particles. You're safe unless you eat the stuff."

"Not hungry. Had lunch already."

She folded her arms and regarded her nominal supervisor with a critical eye. He was a geek and a dork, but he wasn't bad looking. She thought he was smart and, well, kind of sweet.

"Mmm . . . is this thing working?"

"Yup. You bet."

"Can I ask a question?"

Page was taken aback by her unexpected interest. "Sure, fire away."

DuFrayne approached Page's laptop. She readied a finger over the keyboard.

"Right. Here goes. Question is — will my idiotic co-worker ever ask me out for a drink? Or dinner? Or a movie?"

Page, upon hearing the astonishing question, turned pale. He hoped he wasn't going into cardiac arrest.

DuFrayne didn't notice his glassy-eyed stare. Her finger pressed down on the spacebar. Ming raised his eyebrows — another recent coding upgrade — and his reply appeared, one letter after another:

THE WAY IS NOT REVEALED

They both stared at the answer, DuFrayne with annoyance, Page with relief.

"What's that supposed to mean?" she wondered.

"Uhh . . . it's Ming's version of the classic 8-Ball answer — *Ask Again Later.*"

"How much later?"

"Well, he's just a bot, so there's no rule, but probably not now. Probably best to wait a while."

DuFrayne cast her eyes to the ceiling to express derision.

"Some oracle this is . . ."

"Doesn't matter. Ming doesn't know it, but technically I'm your supervisor, and dating is against company policy . . ."

She giggled.

"Technically, that's true."

That evening at Grazella, in the middle of Novato, DuFrayne ordered the shrimp risotto. Page settled for vegetarian lasagna.

The dining room was bathed in romantic lighting, with candles flickering on the tables and wall sconces projecting little stars on the ceiling.

The wine was good, but the conversation was strained.

"Cheers," said DuFrayne. She clicked her glass against his.

Page nodded. He was feeling very uncomfortable. Away from the job, he could not think of a thing to say.

DuFrayne looked across the table at her shy companion. Her eyes were shining in the candle light.

Page looked back. His eyes were wide with something like actual fear. And yet, rolling around in his tongue-tied head was an amazing thought: here he was sharing a meal with a real woman, a woman who was not his grandmother or any other blood relation, a woman who seemed to like what she saw.

They ate in painful silence. Although Page slowly became aware that his dinner partner was kind of pretty, unfortunately his heart was elsewhere. Meanwhile, his inability to engage in ordinary social discourse had him burning with humiliation, and that made him miserably angry.

When the waiter came to carry away their plates, however, Page found the superhuman strength to suggest dessert.

They shared a tiramisu.

Now what? Page agonized over the problem of settling the bill with a proper tip.

"Split the check?" suggested DuFrayne, eyeing Page's pallor. "It's the modern thing to do."

Page agreed with a queasy nod.

"Let's never do this again," he said.

22
00010110

Leo Thorpe and Brava Erpenstock were standing in Karsten Vollmer's cubicle staring at his computer monitor. The elite programmer was demonstrating an early version of Arrowshaft's proposed entry into the bank app market. Thorpe leaned over Vollmer's shoulder, using his finger to navigate the financial landscape. He was impressed by the rapid progress made since a few waves of his arm launched the project.

"Looking good, Kars," said Thorpe.

"We're getting there," returned Vollmer.

"Brava? What do you think?"

Erpenstock folded her arms and tapped a foot.

"We need a title. Without a title we won't move a unit."

"And that's your job, Miss Marketing Manager," reminded Thorpe. "Ideas? I'm listening."

Erpenstock was uncertain. "This is going to take some thought. It's unique, and we need a unique name. I dunno, *Fun with Finance?*"

"Not a chance. It can't seem like a game for kids. People's real money will be on the line."

"Okay, then, let's echo a cliché sports phrase with some muscle — *Take it to the Bank.*"

"Better . . . but . . . well . . ." muttered Thorpe. "It doesn't give me the Big Yes Feeling."

"Look, Leo, I'm vamping here. Let me sit down and have a think."

"Okay, but we need to announce this to Almaden with a catchy word or two. The title is the only thing they will actually understand."

Thorpe gave her a little salute and departed the cubicle. Erpenstock made to follow, but Vollmer stuck out a pudgy arm to stop her.

"Out of my way, you oaf," said she.

"Oaf? I'm an oaf? Listen up, bitch. I need the bank info we talked about. You're the designated hitter on our team, so step up to the plate and go get it."

"I got it already. Let me go."

"Not enough. I need passwords, signatures."

"In case you didn't notice, I'm not in the finance department."

"Too bad, that would make it easy. But I'm pretty sure you'd like to keep that fancy BMW you're driving, and you will find a way. Soon, now. Real soon."

▼

Erpenstock temporized by presenting Ben Seabury with a sheaf of personal receipts for out-of-pocket expenses and, by leaning flirtatiously over his desk, persuading him to write a check to cover them.

"Judy can do this. Where is that woman?"

"Lunch I think."

"Okay, I'll do it. But only if I can take you to dinner tonight," said Seabury.

"Why Ben, I thought you were married. Long-term relationship."

Seabury held up his left hand and wiggled his third finger.

"Do you see a ring?"

Erpenstock laughed. "Gosh, I don't. Dinner it is."

A few minutes later she handed a copy of the check to Karsten Vollmer.

"Here you go, mister. Note the signature — Benjamin R. Seabury, our Chief Financial Officer."

"It's a start," granted the programmer. "Nice work."

23
00010111

In the shipping department, Page and DuFrayne were puzzling over an order for three company T-shirts in sizes small, medium, and large. They were suspicious of the familiar and very strange destination:

```
Rote Königin Medien
Postfach 41 42 D3 56 F3 79 E7 5A
Hannover 30167
DEUTSCHLAND
```

"Postfach?" mumbled DuFrayne.

"German for Post Office Box. I looked it up, just to be sure."

"No one has a box like that."

"Brava confirmed the first one. With those letters mixed in, it looks like hex notation. Maybe it's a P.O. and some kind of routing number."

"What are you talking about? Brava confirmed? Something's up with the babe," declared DuFrayne.

A thought of jealousy, instantly suppressed, ran through Page's mind.

"I'll check again. This is crazy."

Page marched to the elevator, punched a button, and was whisked up to the fourth floor. The elevator door rolled open and started to close again before Page could muster the willpower to step into the beating heart of Arrowshaft Interactive Media.

"Ms. Erpenstock?" he said, peering into the marketing manager's open office door.

"Oliver Page? You look lost. Come in, come in."

He gingerly stepped inside and stretched an arm out toward the marketing manager. The suspect address label was stuck on the end of his forefinger.

"What's this?" she asked, peeling it off for a closer look.

"I don't understand this label. I'm worried that any shipment to an address like this will be lost in transit."

Erpenstock blushed. She recovered her composure by waving the label through the air to simulate its forthcoming intercontinental flight.

"German stuff, Ollie. They do things differently over there."

"I guess so, huh? But I did some checking, and it's completely non-standard."

"Look, the German post office is automated, at least in Hannover. The way it was explained to me, they scan the address for a box number, and then the company scans it to find the right department."

"We do business with these guys?"

"Affirmative. They translate our stuff for European publication."

"Oh. Right. I didn't know."

Erpenstock favored her underling with a dazzling smile, causing Page to lose all sense of his mission.

"Well, thanks for explaining everything," he said. "I'll make sure the package moves tonight."

"Thank *you,* Ollie, for being so conscientious."

24
00011000

On the other side of the country, in the Friendship Annex of the National Security Agency, Warren Ash was staring at his computer monitors while chatting with his supervisor via an encrypted intercom app.

"I'm baffled, Sandy," said Ash. He was holding a pair of small iron cannonballs, souvenirs of a Mini Cooper tour through Civil War monuments in Pennsylvania. His arms were outstretched, and between sentences he was lifting the spheres high overhead, working out.

"Nutcracker did a first pass without result," he reported. "Mouse King says further processing will tap our budget for seventy-five thousand dollars, and no guarantee."

Alexander Ufford was not pleased to hear the news. "Jesus Christ. The key we have is 64-bit, ready for the cracking. This is ridiculous."

"What is it?" wheezed Ash. "Air gap isolation with a jumper? SHA code? Some dumb RSA keychain deal?"

"If that were true we'd be reading the plain text."

"Yeah . . ." — another wheeze as Ash lifted his weights — "so it's gotta be a one-time pad."

"Either that or the Nutcracker team is mining bitcoin instead of decoding our traffic."

"Right on, boss. And get this, I'm seeing probe after probe into Almaden Capital Management. Sooner or later, trouble is coming."

"We don't know for sure."

"Trust me, Sandy, I've got my legendary feeling."

"Your feeling . . . that and a dollar . . ."

"Look at it this way — we pursue the problem as research for now, show the Mouse King how the big boys strut their stuff, and look for another key. Accumulate and analyze" — Ash huffed and puffed through a final weight lift — "at Almaden's expense, not ours, ha ha."

25
00011001

Page was having dinner with Fillmore and Hoffman at their usual spot, the Puerto Seguro café. Tonight the air was warm, and the three of them were out on the patio, eating flautas and drinking Mexican beer while they hammered away at their indie game.

Since their last get-together, Hoffman had created scary little monsters in two forms: aliens and zombies.

"Which do you like?" she inquired. "We should choose one or the other before I take this any further."

Fillmore was deferential. "I like the aliens. But, you're the artist, you tell us."

Hoffman waggled her head uncertainly. "The zombies are scarier."

Page spread his arms. "Let's do both. We can show a selection screen, let the users pick. It's the same game."

Hoffman turned to Fillmore. "That would be cool. Can do?"

Fillmore nodded. "It's not even hard, as long as the sprite metrics stay the same. I can even vary the attack pattern AI without much trouble."

"Except," complained Hoffman, "then we need a generic title."

"We don't have any title yet," noted Page. "But I've been thinking. What about *Personal Defense?*"

Hoffman frowned. "Um . . . sounds like pepper spray."

"Okay, then, *Fatal Footsteps.*"

"Too murder mystery."

"Mutazoids?"

Fillmore stirred. "I like the *zoids* part."

"But I think it's taken," confessed Page. He stared at his uneaten beans. "But wait — we could use *Aggrozoids.* You know, aggressive, but generic. Zombies, aliens, both work."

"Hey, not bad, Ollie," allowed Fillmore.

"But we've got to get *defenses* in there somehow," insisted Hoffman. "It spells out the type of game, when the monsters are all coming at you."

"So, we call it *Aggrozoid Defenders,* how's that?"

Hoffman and Fillmore exchanged approving glances.

"For now. Unless we get a brain wave."

Fillmore stood up from the table. He drained off his beer and dropped a pile of bills beside his plate. He patted Hoffman's hand. "I'm outa here. Laundry night."

Hoffman remained seated. Page watched him go, brow furrowed in total confusion.

"I thought you two were, you know, like together or something."

Hoffman smiled. "We are. But we keep our own apartments."

"I see," said Page. He didn't. "Can I ask you something?"

"Shoot."

"I'm sending out packages, and every so often I mail some dumb trinket to Germany, to some company called *Rote Königin Medien.* How would you figure out what's going on over there?"

Hoffman considered the problem. *"Rote Königin."* she repeated. She seemed disturbed by the foreign name. "What's it mean? In English?"

"Red Queen Media, according to Google."

"Aha. Well, in Germany? You publish over there? Who does your localization?"

"Our what?"

"Who translates your games into German?"

"I don't know."

"Find out and ask him. Might know. Maybe Red Queen is the guy's own company."

26
00011010

In the morning, once the latest arriving shipments were unboxed, once all the latest orders were filled, and once all the toys and T-shirts were inventoried and stacked on their respective shelves, Page left the department and ascended to the fourth floor with questions for Brava Erpenstock.

He knew he would be dazzled just to be in the presence of the beautiful marketing woman, and he vowed to overcome his awkwardness with a careful rehearsal in the men's room before approaching her.

"Morning, Ms. Erpenstock," he said, hewing to his internal script, "I've got a question."

Erpenstock looked up at her underling. She was not amused by his obvious nerves, which made her uncomfortably self-conscious. Her eyes narrowed. "Go ahead," she said.

"I was wondering if . . . if you had the name of whoever it is who translates our game text into German."

"Why do you want to know?"

"Well, I studied German in college," — he forced out the planned lie — "and I was just curious . . . might be a good contact back and forth."

Erpenstock shook her head decisively. "I don't think that's a good idea, Page. We've got channels, it all goes through Leo's design group."

He noticed that she casually closed a loose-leaf notebook on her desk as she spoke.

"Unh-huh, I see. Makes a lot of sense. Pardon me for disturbing you."

"Oh no problem. Anytime." Her tone conveyed a less friendly meaning. Page winced and retreated.

▼

Distaste for Page's unwanted attention wasn't the only reason for Erpenstock's cool demeanor. Vollmer was after her again, and she was entirely focused on saving herself from prosecution by satisfying the man's illegal requests.

Her chosen tactic was an intimate conversation with Judy Hagen, Ben Seabury's financial assistant.

"Hey, girl, I need some numbers."

"What kind of numbers?"

"I don't even know the budget for my own department. I need to make intelligent decisions on how to spend a strictly limited amount of money."

"Gee, Brava, I don't know. Talk to Ben."

"I did already. He and Magowan — *sheesh* — if I don't generate some customer awareness, and pronto, we'll be out of our jobs."

"The rumor mill is buzzing. Is it that bad?"

"Worse. Potential bankruptcy."

Hagen blanched.

"How about this? Work late tonight. I'll leave my office unlocked when I leave."

"Sounds like a plan. We're going to save Ben's ass in spite of himself."

▼

Page was also working late, or at least giving that impression to his colleague DuFrayne, who packed up her bag and departed at six o'clock on the dot with a sharp "See ya."

When the late spring sun was well down he ventured out into the main lobby, where most of the lights were off. He was relieved to find that the receptionist was gone for the day. He knew that the janitors only made their rounds on alternate nights, and not on this one. The feeling of being alone buoyed his spirits, put a spring in his step as he marched across the reception area and decisively pressed the elevator button.

He stepped out into the fourth-floor corridor in almost total darkness. Tiny LEDs revealed the location of electrical outlets and not much else. Light from the City of Novato and cars on the Redwood Highway spilled in through the building's tall windows. All in all, Page had just enough illumination to prevent himself from crashing into decorative plants, water fountains, and printing stations.

Glancing sideways into the sea of cubicles revealed a task light glowing on someone's desk — a junior programmer crunching on some impossible deadline, no doubt.

He inched past the conference room in the opposite direction, rounded a corner, and stopped cold. A little headlight a few inches above the floor was approaching. As he stood in place with his pulse racing, a robot sweeper shaped like a frisbee bumped against his feet, appeared to consider the unusual obstacle, then detoured around him and continued on its automatic way.

He slowly walked the corridor, looking for Erpenstock's office. Using the flashlight on his smartphone, he read the sign on a door about halfway along: *Marketing.* The door was open, a condition he was hoping for, but unsure about. The interior itself was barely lit by a single night light behind the desk, turning ordinary workplace shapes into eerie monstrosities. He eased inside, then halted. Wait a minute. Something further along the corridor tickled his eye. Inside another office, flashes of light were throwing someone's shadow into the hall.

He thought it would be prudent to investigate and stealthily worked his way into position for a look inside.

"Ooh . . ." he gasped.

There in Judy Hagen's office, Brava Erpenstock was recklessly opening and closing cupboards and drawers, then photographing her finds. Her blond hair glimmered in the flashes from her smartphone's camera. She seemed agitated. She was obviously searching for something. Just as obviously, her search was no more legitimate than his own.

Page absorbed the discovery as a heavy blow. Something fishy about the Arrowshaft marketing maid, he suddenly realized. Connecting the dots, he also understood why Erpenstock's own office was unlocked. He tiptoed back the way he came, dodged back into that office, turned on his smartphone's flashlight, and ran it over her desk, looking for the loose-leaf notebook he had spotted earlier in the day.

He was in a near panic and ready to bolt when his hand touched the binder he was seeking, tucked in among a line of business books. He opened it and thumbed through the sell sheets and cost schedules until he came to a brochure advertising *Localization.* There he spotted a foreign name:

Helmut Osterwald

The corporate address was listed in Hamburg, Germany. There was a telephone number. Page snapped a photo with his own smartphone camera and closed the notebook. He hurried out of the office and back along the corridor toward the elevator, nearly tripping over another mindless sweeperbot whirring along the floor.

Just before calling for his ride back down to familiar territory, he looked back over his shoulder and saw Erpenstock returning from Hagen's office.

Uh-oh, what if she saw light from the elevator car when the doors opened? Page's finger froze inches from the button. He continued down the corridor to the fire exit. Then, when he was sure Erpenstock had turned into her office, he shoved the door open, clattered down the stairs, and escaped.

27
00011011

"Helmut Osterwald?"

"Ja . . ." A German voice.

"Oh, hello. My name is Oliver Page. I work at Arrowshaft Interactive."

"From the States." The voice switched instantly into unaccented English.

"That's right. You translated *Combo Warriors* for us, right?"

"Yes. *Jawoll.* I did. And all your sick *Pony* games for little girls."

"Man, am I glad I found you."

Page had awakened two hours before dawn, wrestling with the implications of his secret nighttime expedition to the fourth floor and Brava Erpenstock's off-limits foray. He was worried about her, and he was becoming obsessed with crazy German post office box numbers.

He wanted answers and good advice on a course of action, so he opened his laptop, fired up his chatbot, rubbed his eyes, and asked an important question:

"Hey there, Mighty Ming — should I just forget everything I saw, or should I keep going, stay on the trail of . . . who knows what? Something dark and dirty, that's for sure."

The bearded bot hummed thoughtfully, and his advice appeared below his head:

THE SUPERIOR MAN IS FIRMLY RESOLVED

Thus encouraged, Page turned to Skype and called Osterwald during Germany's business day, nine hours ahead of U.S. Pacific Coast time.

"May I ask you a question?"

"Please."

"I do a lot of shipping. Toys, mugs, packaged goods, and I've seen several pieces heading for a German post office box number in Hannover that is sixteen digits long in hexadecimal notation. What kind of P.O. box is that?"

"Numbered in *hex?*" Osterwald was incredulous. "None here . . . none in Hannover . . . none anywhere. Such a thing is crazy."

"That's what I think. Another question?"

"Okay . . ."

"The addressee on these shipping labels is 'Rote Konigin Medien.' Mean anything? Is it a studio? Arrowshaft partner or something?"

"Königin, Königin," repeated Osterwald, emphasizing the umlaut over the 'o' that Page could not pronounce.

"Well . . ?"

"Red Queen? I have not heard of them."

"Can you check around for me?"

"Tell me your email, I'll send a note."

Page gave him his company address and ended the call with profuse thanks.

Later that morning he was biking to work with his mind in turmoil, so distracted that he hardly noticed the woman in the lime green helmet when she flew past him on her carbon fiber road rocket. As she pedaled into the distance he refocused.

"Hey," he shouted, "when is that century you're training for?"

She didn't hear him.

▼

In the Arrowshaft shipping department Page helped Emilee Du-Frayne unload a dozen crates full of *Pony Corral* activity books.

"What's going on with Ms. Erpenstock?" he wondered.

"Who cares?" sneered DuFrayne. "Oh, I forgot — you do."

"Come on, this might be important. I saw her looking for stuff in an office that doesn't belong to her. She's in management, has the run of the place. Why sneak around?"

"Maybe she's not the nice person you admire so much," said Du-Frayne.

"Or . . ." mused Page, "maybe she's under the gun. Maybe someone is making her do bad things."

"Oh please."

"If I can figure it out, I could get her out of trouble. Save her."

DuFrayne studied Page for signs of mental damage. *"Save her?* The last time anyone worshipped a woman like you worship the Erpenbabe was in Thomas Hardy novels. Bathsheba Everdene, a million years ago."

"Who?"

"Sorry, I was an English major. Probably why I have no real job skills."

▼

Just before closing time, Page discovered an email from Germany in his inbox:

> *Oliver:*
>
> *No one over here has ever heard of Rote Königin. Definitely not any kind of company in the game business. Hacker group?*
>
> *— Helmut O*

28
00011100

In the NSA's Friendship Annex outside Baltimore, Alexander Ufford got a phone call that sent him scurrying through the forest of cubicles to Warren Ash's corner.

"Warren — !"

"Hey, Sandy, I'm getting hot on the one-time pad I've been tracking. I've got a MAC address on the American machine, and I've got the outlines of a pattern. Hacker flaw? Maybe so. When the evildoers update, it looks like some of the digits repeat, just shifted over."

"Forget your Dutch bank hackers, Warren."

"What? Why? We can exploit this."

Ufford made a time out gesture. "Negatory, Mr. Ash. Stand down. I just got word — someone is probing into the Central Valley Project out in CA, looking to open the gates of Folsom Dam and flood Sacramento. They issued an anonymous threat.'"

"Are you serious?"

"Very."

"Shit, who we got?"

"That's your job. Figure it out."

"Yessir, boss."

Ash tapped his screen to clear away the routine surveillance and typed in a series of search terms to aim Air Traffic Control at the more pressing problem. After five minutes of scrutiny, no plausible device was actively trying to make contact with Folsom Dam's hydraulic systems.

"I don't see anything, Sandy."

Ufford threw up his hands.

"Keep an eye peeled. Call me the moment you spot trouble."

"Sure, you bet."

Ufford patted Ash on the shoulder and returned to his office.

Ash continued to watch the tags on his screen advance upward, but when, after another fifteen minutes without the slightest indication of a plot to flood California's Big Valley, he switched back to monitor the ongoing attempts to penetrate Rabobank. He was well aware that the dam was a more important and urgent situation, but he was fascinated by the clever encryption scheme that had so far defeated all his team's decoding efforts.

Ash picked up his cannon balls and began lifting weights while he considered the small clues and possibilities.

>>> 0100

PART FOUR

150

29
00011101

Doyle Magowan, Ben Seabury, Leo Thorpe, and Brava Erpenstock were gathered in Karsten Vollmer's cubicle for a demo of Arrowshaft's proposed financial app in *Beta* form.

Vollmer ran through the features with a voice-over commentary. All were impressed by the rapid progress of development.

"What's real and what's staged?" wondered Seabury.

"It's all real," declared Vollmer. "No polish, but all the elements are in. If we had real clients, we could do real transactions."

"Why not add the company bank?" suggested Erpenstock. "Then we have something to show off."

"That's a great idea," affirmed Vollmer. He gave the marketing lady a sly grin.

"Put High Beam in there, while you're at it," continued Erpenstock. "We owe my consulting guys a payment. Might as well make it when you demo to the owners."

Seabury jingled the change in his pocket. "Okay. We show those guys we're not demonstrating vaporware."

Magowan poked a finger at the screen. "Name, Brava? What are we going to call this thing?"

Erpenstock folded her arms. "That's a tough one. Remember, we're not selling this to the public at large. It's for commercial customers. Gotta be informative."

"Inform me," commanded Magowan.

"Virtual Finance?"

Magowan shook his head. "Sounds like a toy. Buyers will be looking for real finance."

"How about *Financial Footsteps?* You know, signal the 3D aspects explicitly."

Thorpe frowned. "Makes our stuff sound slow. No go."

"Oh for God's sake. My last idea — *Money Matters 360.* "

Magowan's glum demeanor perked up. "That's better. Money does matter. Why not 365 — every day?"

"Because, Doyle," Erpenstock declared with some heat, *"360* is our way of proclaiming 3D, our virtual world, and so on." Her cheeks were red.

Magowan pulled a handkerchief out of his pocket and waved the white flag. "Okay, okay, we go with it for now."

▼

In San Francisco, Magowan and Seabury cooled their heels in the Almaden Capital Management conference room for twenty minutes before Albert Weisbrod joined them.

"Gentlemen," said the lawyer. "What have you got for me?"

Magowan opened a leather case and extracted an oversize laptop computer.

"I have here a demo version of AIM's new financial application for PCs and mobile devices. *Money Matters 360.*"

"I like the title anyway," granted Weisbrod.

Magowan placed the computer on the conference room table, opened the lid, and turned it on.

"Ben, do the honors? You're better at this than I am."

Seabury dutifully ran through the demo. He even walked down the virtual street from Arrowshaft's virtual Rabobank branch and made a real payment from Arrowshaft's account to the account of High Beam Consulting.

Weisbrod watched enigmatically until Seabury concluded his presentation. Then: "How do we make our money? This is for corporate buyers, yes?"

Seabury nodded. "That's right. We'll sell subscriptions, and we'll service advertisements. Cool ones, up on virtual billboards. We'll also authorize online retailers to lease real estate on our virtual premises. And finally, we will collect and aggregate users' financial data — anonymously of course — and sell it to interested parties. The banks take a cut, and we take the rest."

"And how long does this arrangement last?"

Magowan cleared his throat. "That would be forever, Albert."

Weisbrod spread his arms wide. "I am impressed. I will show this to Mr. Nazari and Mr. Karnovsky. I am sure they will be equally impressed."

Magowan made a tiny bow. "I hope so. They should be."

Weisbrod raised a threatening finger. His voice became cold. "Your app is cute. The name is catchy. But the test is still to come. No *Alpha*, no *Beta*. Just . . . what do you call it when you ship?"

"Golden Master."

"Yes, ha ha. Golden. Show us some revenue."

30
00011110

Page spent the last hour of his workday at the shipping department desk tweaking the AI on his virtual monster swarm. He was prepping for a meetup with Karen Hoffman and Jimmy Fillmore to bring the indie video game they were all developing — *Aggrozoid Defenders* — to *Alpha*.

DuFrayne was gathering her things to leave, but couldn't resist a curious peek over his shoulder.

"Hey, that's not your so-called chatbot for a change. What now?" she wondered.

Page performed a quick compile of his code and showed her a view of little squares dancing around the shipping department floor and gradually approaching the laptop screen.

"I'm working on the AI. We can't actually show occlusion, if a monster gets behind a chair, see? But if I move these little dudes side-to-side on their way, it looks like they're avoiding obstacles."

"What's AI?"

"Artificial intelligence — NPC goals, how they move to achieve them. A-star, basically."

"What's an NPC? What's A-star?"

"NPC is a non-player character. A-star is a search algorithm for route planning. Geez, Duffy. Ever play a game?"

"Hearts . . ."

Page gulped. "Yeah, cards are cool. See you tomorrow."

▼

In the Meadowlands shopping center near the freeway, the Puerto Seguro café was slammed at happy hour. Page surveyed the customers. No Fillmore, no Hoffman. For a moment he was at a loss. Then he walked a block to the Butterfly, and there they were.

"Hey, bro, coffee tonight instead of Negra Modelo," grinned Fillmore. "Whatcha got for us?"

Page hauled out his laptop and showed off his new AI.

"Excellent, pardner. It actually looks like those little fuckers are right here in our augmented fucking reality. Give me your machine."

"Huh?"

"No Wi-Fi here tonight," explained Fillmore.

Page handed over his laptop, and Fillmore connected it to his own computer with a USB cable.

"What's the folder name?"

"Uh, Swarm_Workfiles."

"Got it."

Fillmore copied the files.

"Whoa there, did you know your Windows build is like, what? Two revs out of date?"

Page frowned. "What are you doing? Keep your fingers out of my operating system."

"Sure, just checking."

He pulled the plug and returned the laptop.

While Page and Hoffman loaded up on caffeine and pastries, Fillmore merged their code and art assets on his own laptop. Fifteen minutes later the game was running on his smartphone. The three of them ran through the selection screens and watched as the swarm of monsters materialized in the far corners of the café, then marched across the floor toward them.

Hoffman feigned alarm. "Shoot!" she ordered.

Fillmore pressed a button on the smartphone's glass face.

"Pew-pew!" he chirped, as a laser-simulating missile issued from the screen and obliterated the nearest alien attackers. *"Pew-pew!"*

"Tah-dah. Congratulations, men," glowed Hoffman. "No sound effects yet, unless we want to record Jimmy here. But all our other elements are in."

Page was staring at his screen, suspiciously making sure his laptop was undamaged, and that Fillmore's casual usage was not some kind of casual abuse. "Guys, I have Wi-Fi. Here's Google News."

Fillmore peeked over his shoulder. "Look at that — I guess the network came back up, huh?"

"Are you sure it went down at all?"

Fillmore waved a hand. "I couldn't see it on my machine. Maybe I need to restart the damn thing."

"Wi-Fi, Schmi-Fi. We have *Alpha!* " declared Hoffman. "We need alcohol to celebrate, not coffee. We must march."

With that the three proud indie game developers walked back to Puerto Seguro. Happy hour was over, and the crowd had thinned. They sat down in a booth and ordered beers.

"Here's something that's bothering me," ventured Page. "I've been shipping stuff to Germany, to an Arrowshaft partner that doesn't exist at a P.O. box that doesn't make sense."

"What are you talking about?" queried Fillmore.

"Ever hear of *Rote Königin Medien?* Or a P.O. box numbered in *hex?*"

Fillmore scowled. "W-T-F, bro?"

"I don't know. That's why I'm asking."

Hoffman shrugged. "Beats me."

Page pursed his lips. "I called our localization specialist over there. He thinks Red Queen Media might be a hacker collective."

"And you're shipping toys to them?"

"What it looks like. And they do not get returned from the ridiculous sixteen-digit addresses on our labels, which I think is a code."

"A code?" scoffed Fillmore. "You've been reading too many Sherlock Holmes stories."

"No I haven't. Let's say it really is a code. Sixteen hex digits.

How would that work?"

Fillmore swigged his beer. He put the bottle down on the table and turned it slowly round and round. He was thinking.

"Hash values, SHA codes, — the keys that hackers use — are really long, sixty-four digits in hex. So your code is way too simple. It's some kind of mistake, or just a twenty-first century address that does, like, pre-sorting. You know, takes in the company, which building, what floor, the right department, et cetera."

Page was not persuaded.

"How about a one-time pad? I transmit the latest page, a few messages go back and forth somewhere, then that code is obsolete, and there I am sending another one. The toys and trinkets are just an excuse for the labels."

"You're fantasizing, bro," insisted Fillmore. "You want a hack? Take a look at this . . ."

He aimed the browser on his laptop at a game website and pointed to an advertisement running along the right-hand margin:

Coming To Get You Soon
AGGROZOID DEFENDERS
Stop them before they eat your phone!

The text was decorated with little versions of Hoffman's aliens and zombies. Page was stunned.

"Is this a real site? Is this live?"

"It's real. It's live. Our discovery problem — solved!"

"How are you doing this? Ads cost money, Jimmy."

"Well now, let's just say I piggybacked on a company account."

"Oh man, what company?"

Fillmore grinned. "You don't want to know."

"Not Arrowshaft! Jesus Christ, Jimmy."

"I didn't say that. Take it easy."

"How many spots did you buy with someone else's money?"

"It's running on the top ten game sites," said Hoffman.

"Oh my God!" moaned Page.

"We need to get recognized," insisted Hoffman. "It's our only hope, Ollie."

Page was generally deferential to his more experienced collaborators, but this issue realigned his moral compass, drifting after a year in the game biz, awakening ethical outrage.

"Listen to me, you two," he growled. "Especially you, James. I'm not going to work with hackers. It's fraud, it's theft, it's dishonest, and it's most likely criminal." He blinked. The ferocity of his views surprised him as much as it did his friends.

Fillmore shook his head, inclined to take pity on his naïve young partner.

"Criminal, really?"

"Whatever. You can't be doing this shit. No more."

Fillmore sat back in his chair. He downed the last of his beer.

"Okay, pal. You're right. It's petty theft. We'll find another way."

"No kidding, Jimmy. This is a big deal."

Fillmore grimaced.

"Message delivered. Hitting the reset button, amigo."

31
00011111

Page spent the next few days in a trance. Incoming boxes piled up, and outgoing shipments stalled, causing DuFrayne to moan and groan.

"Ollie . . ."

"I know, I know."

"Know what, if you don't mind telling me — what's with you, anyway?"

"Rote Königin."

"Sounds German. I studied French in school."

"It means *Red Queen.* Why red? Why queen?"

DuFrayne was already walking away. She stopped short.

"She's a character in *Alice Through the Looking-Glass.*"

Page had never read the classic tale, but he suddenly felt like he was falling down a rabbit hole.

"Oh, right. A book. It's all part of the code we're staring at on our shipping labels."

Page stood up from his desk. He sleepwalked to the department workbench and began boxing and wrapping the pile of merchandising goods that had accumulated there. His hands moved automatically, assembling boxes, filling them, slapping on tape while his mind drifted toward half a dozen conspiracy theories.

DuFrayne was alarmed by his strange behavior. "Earth calling Page . . ?"

"Oh, listen, Duff — what if someone here at AIM is involved with a bunch of hackers? And we're involved, sending their codes."

He aimed a finger at the department's printer.

"Print me out all our German labels, would you?"

DuFrayne placed her hands on her hips. "Say please."

"Please."

Page peeled the reprinted labels free of their waxy backing and stuck them in chronological order on the workbench surface.

"See, Duff, those numbers after *postfach?* Hexadecimal. They represent sixty-four binary digits. What do we think? How does the code work?"

DuFrayne tugged at a lock of hair. "By boring us to death."

"The P.O. box on each label is completely different. But each one is sixty-four digits. Looks to me like a one-time pad . . ."

"What is that? My pad has two rooms."

"It's the key to a special kind of code. Users just write a few messages, then throw it away."

"Why shipping labels? Why not email the thing?"

"One-time pads are unbreakable. Unless the key gets intercepted. Email isn't secure. But who notices shipping labels? At least, that's my theory . . ."

"In theory everything works."

". . . and the question then becomes, how do the bad guys generate their pads?"

"A riddle inside a mystery . . ."

"I think — sixty-four digits — they could be using the same generator I use, my Mersenne Twister."

"Your what? Sounds like a pop song trend."

Page ran a finger over the zip codes.

"But that's not the whole story. I just noticed — the postal codes are all different. I don't understand."

"What I don't understand is, how come the packages got delivered and not returned?"

Page turned to his co-worker. "That, Ms. DuFrayne, is a very good question."

▼

Page sat down at the desk, opened up his laptop, and wrote an email to the German translator:

Helmut:

Arrowshaft Fulfillment here. How come our packages, each with a different postfach and zip code, don't get returned? Any ideas?"

— *Oliver*

A reply was waiting when he arrived for work next morning:

Oliver:

Possibly the recipient works in the central office, before mail gets sorted by zip, and collects your packages there.

— *Helmut O*

Yes, that was a possibility. Page thought it likely.

With that working hypothesis running through his head, he biked to the Novato public library, where he looked up an edition of Lewis Carrol's *Through the Looking-Glass, and What Alice Found There.*

What Page found there were numerous mentions of a Red Queen, first as a chess piece, then as a very peculiar and disagreeable human character.

It occurred to Page as he skimmed through the ridiculous book that he was becoming obsessed by shipping labels.

▼

"Hey, Jimmy. Sorry about my tirade."

"That's okay, bro. You stood up for your what you believe."

A week had gone by since the *Aggrozoid* creators' last meetup. Page was still feeling the tension that erupted and thought a telephone call was the easiest way to renew contact with his friends. So he dialed up Fillmore from the safe distance of his garage in Petaluma.

"Here's why I'm calling . . . crazy P.O. boxes aren't the only weird numbers on my labels. Each one shows a slightly different zip code. Probably part of the encryption scheme."

"Could be," allowed Fillmore. "Hard to tell, though. That's why codes work — it's tough to figure them out."

"Understood. But let's say Red Queen means something. She's a character in *Alice.* Could you use the book she's in to improve a lousy sixty-four-digit one-time pad?"

Fillmore was silent for a long moment.

"Jimmy — ?"

"I'm here. Think *salt.*"

"Salt?"

"That's what your serious codemeisters call it. You want to make a code unbreakable? Add salt. Pick some extra factor, add it to your stew, hash it, and *zap!* you've got a gourmet meal."

"Salt. That's what I do to make true random numbers — add little bits from the real world. Colors, clocks, radioactivity, that kind of stuff."

Fillmore was silent again. Page thought the connection was lost, but no: "Your labels are crazy? Know how *you* sound, Ollie? Why do you give a shit about this crap?"

Yeah, why? The query forced Page's loose curiosity to shape itself into actual suspicion.

"I think someone here at Arrowshaft is on some hacking team hacking something. That's why. Don't know what."

Fillmore laughed.

"Man, you are one deranged paranoid dude. Run right out and hire a shrink, you need one."

"Whoa there . . ."

"Or, better yet, talk to Ming. He'll set you straight, ha ha."

32
00100000

Warm weather arrived in June.

The occasional heavy storms that fouled winter and spring turned to sprinkles now and then, and finally, in the last weeks of May, all clouds were banished from the Northern California sky. Spring grass, sprouting green and tall along the bike path from SMART to work, withered and turned golden brown. The muddy little sloughs meandering toward San Pablo Bay dried out.

Time for another ascent of Mount Burdell.

On this trip, working his mountain bike hard in low gears, Page managed to reach the summit without stepping off even once.

He laid his ride on the grass, sat down, and spent half an hour taking in the view. Way to the south he could see a thick tongue of fog rolling in through the Golden Gate, moisture sucked from the ocean by inland heat.

He revved up his smartphone and composed a message:

> *Hi Mom, Hi Gram:*
>
> *All good here in CA. New friends, 2 jobs. Ware is soft, work is hard. Fun anyway.*
>
> *xoxo — OP*

He was responding to repeated emails from the older generations, all expressing worry about their blood kin dying a slow and lonely death on the soul-crushing West Coast.

With family obligations held at bay, he was faced with a personal emptiness and nothing to fill it, except to ruminate on his career. The company he worked for was staggering. He didn't know why, but the rumor mill was grinding out unpleasant possibilities. And somewhere within the shaky organization someone was busy perpetrating fraud. The purpose of such treachery eluded him, even as the mere idea made his blood boil.

Another problem, possibly as worrisome — his good friend Jimmy Fillmore was evidently some kind of hacker himself. Page was starting to regret having given the guy direct access to his laptop. He was pretty sure the Butterfly network was working just fine the whole time the three developers were in there. That meant there was something sly about Fillmore's request to connect with cables. He told himself to run a malware scan on his computer as soon as possible, just in case Fillmore was up to something unthinkable.

He felt helpless to affect the swirl of events, and the feeling made him queasy. Self-pity? No, he assured himself, he was responding to reality. He was demonstrably helpless. Helpless and hopeless.

His thoughts turned to his childish coping mechanisms. Relying on his chatbot to steer a course through life suddenly filled him with self-loathing.

"Grow up!" he said aloud.

Then he mounted his bike and bounced back down the mountainside to the winding roads and strip malls and housing developments of greater Novato.

Back home he opened a beer, opened his laptop, and prepared to revise some of Ming's chatbot advice. Armed with the fearsome thought that he must eventually advance beyond the silly computer program he depended on, he decided a nudge in the right direction was in order. Accordingly, he removed Ming's ambiguous answer number 2 — *Clouds Gather* — which, after all, was very similar to ambiguous answer number 1 — *Smoke Fills The Sky* — and replaced it with a telegraphic manifesto . . .

Deeds Demand Doing

Then, in an even more drastic move, he replaced Ming's ambiguous answer number 3 — *Fate Is Uncertain* — which was equally repetitive, with a stern commandment he remembered from the Bible and his childhood catechism classes . . .

Put Away Childish Things

He fervently hoped that his chatbot code, tweaked and prodded into mysterious true randomness, would not reach into his life from beyond ordinary reality and cause either of these messages to answer any of his questions anytime in the near future.

But he wanted to be ready.

33
00100001

All the following day, Page was consumed by impulses and doubts. Impulses to investigate his suspicions about hacking within the company, and doubts about risking his job to do so.

He was trying to resolve the issue intelligently, as an adult, by quietly pursuing the clues.

First, he ran a scan of his personal laptop, looking for signs of malicious software lurking there. No threats were found, easing his mind about Fillmore. The results made him feel guilty for having so much as imagined a breach of trust.

Next, he wanted to find out who sent the peculiar German mailing addresses to the shipping department computer for printing.

They all came from Brava Erpenstock, and he doubted she was actually hacking anything. He focused on the most recent message, which he had not previously seen. He guessed that DuFrayne must have printed the label. Unlike the others, he saw that it was forwarded in haste from another message, and the originating address block was still visible:

```
From: karvol@arrowintermed.com
Sent: 06/23, 9:30A
To: brave@arrowintermed.com
Subject: ship item
```

Page felt his arms tingle. He was looking at a hacker possibility. But who was *karvol?*

He waited for DuFrayne to leave for the day, then reached into the department desk for a printed copy of the company roster, and sifted through the alphabet. Nothing under *A* or *K* or *R,* but under *V* he spotted the name, *Vollmer.*

"Aha!" he exclaimed.

The name was familiar; he had heard it on the company gossip wire and was vaguely aware that Vollmer was the man hired for the programming job Page himself wanted. A pleasant vision of ironic revenge pranced through his head before he rejected the thought as unworthy.

Evening was approaching. Almost everyone would soon have left the building. If he dared another secret foray into the corporate jungle, would it be possible to get some evidence to back up his suspicions? He knew Vollmer must work somewhere up on the fourth floor, but where? In an office? In a cube? What if the guy was working all night?

Page resolved to make the effort, disdaining his chatbot, when his doubts suddenly overwhelmed his impulses.

He groaned.

"Who am I kidding? This idea sucks, and I'm a jerk," he sighed. He rose from his desk and stalked around the department weighing the possibilities.

"I was almost caught last time," he recalled.

He stumbled to the workbench and spent half an hour slathering tape over cardboard boxes, getting a jump on tomorrow's shipments.

"On the other hand, this might be my big chance," he mumbled. "Ming, where are you, I need advice . . ."

Defeated in his attempt at adulthood, Page opened his laptop and consulted his wise old sage.

"All right, Dr. M, can't decide. What do you think? Should I risk a trip upstairs? Give it a try?"

Master Ming hummed and blinked and waggled his beard . . .

DEEDS DEMAND DOING

Whoa! One of Ming's new messages, superstitiously installed to force personal growth (and much feared for that reason), was staring at Page. He gasped.

An hour and a half later the summer sun was well down, twilight was fading, and night was upon Arrowshaft Interactive Media. Page summoned the elevator and rode it up to the fourth floor.

Aside from guide lights here and there, the place was dark. He turned on his smartphone flashlight and made his way cautiously along the corridor, checking each office as he moved. All were locked up tight, and none displayed a sign for Vollmer.

He turned around and hiked to the other side of the building and into what seemed like an acre of open cubicles, divided into rows by narrow aisles.

He was stealthily checking each one in a methodical search pattern when he heard the elevator doors slide open. A shaft of light appeared in the corridor, and a heavy man's shadow fell on the opposite wall. Page killed his flashlight.

In another moment the heavy man himself was striding toward the cubicle farm. Page ducked down and squirmed under a desk. He held his breath.

The man turned into a cubicle one aisle over, sat down with a groan, turned on a task light, and began typing noisily. This went on for twenty minutes, accompanied by wheezy murmurings that Page could not make out.

Then, in a louder voice, he heard *"Willkommen in Amerika, meine Freunde."*

Switches popped, a cooling fan spun down, the task light snapped off. The man heaved himself out of his chair and threaded his way out of the work station maze and back to the elevator.

Page painfully unfolded himself from his hiding place and peered over the cubicle rim. Light streamed into the corridor briefly as the elevator doors opened, then closed. The heavy man was gone.

But not forgotten: "Vollmer!" said Page, "Gotta be."

He crept into the nearest aisle, tiptoed to the end, and then back along the next aisle, shining his flashlight into every cube he passed.

The voice he had heard could only be coming from one or two of the cubes he was exploring. And only one of them had a screensaver running on a computer. Page eased into the cluttered space, sat in the recently vacated chair, which was still warm, grabbed the computer's mouse, and pressed the left button. The screensaver disappeared and a black banner emblazoned with bold white letters appeared over a view of some unrecognizable European city:

ZUTRITT VERBOTEN

The language was German, Page knew, even though he had never studied it. So, the cubicle belonged to that guy Vollmer. Was Vollmer a German citizen, he wondered, or more likely, an American born in Germany? Either way, Page was sure he had found the Arrowshaft hacker.

He turned his flashlight on the cubby walls, where Vollmer had tacked up sheets of paper. Page was puzzled by the lists scrawled there. They looked like bank IDs and credit card numbers. The words *SWIFT, IBAN, USD,* and *EUROS* appeared alongside some of the entries.

"Oh my God . . ." he muttered. He was convinced that he had caught Vollmer worming his way into the nation's bank accounts.

"Wait, what's this?"

Turning his flashlight to the side revealed a bubble diagram sketched on another sheet of paper. The crudely drawn circles and arrows mapped a sequence of user controls for a mobile app. Along the top margin Page read the words, *Money Matters 360.*

"Ah, shit," he grumped.

Vollmer must be programming the company's new financial app. No wonder he had lists of bank accounts and credit cards.

Page sighed. All that angst, all that work, all those cramps — all for nothing. He stood up wearily, pressing a hand against his sore spine.

Just then Vollmer's screensaver kicked back in. The image of a cruise ship lit up the engineer's computer screen and faded into a skyscraper. The skyscraper gave way to a busty nude woman. The woman cut to a *Star Wars* droid, and the droid dissolved into the close-up photo of a classical chess piece.

Page sat back down. He looked closely at the image. The piece was made from straight-grained wood, turned on a lathe, and stained red. The little circlet crown carved on top left no doubt — he was looking at the picture of a red queen.

34
00100010

Page woke up at dawn and rode his bike to the Petaluma SMART Station in time to catch an early southbound train. Once aboard, he bought coffee at the snack bar, dropped into a window seat, and stared indifferently at the soggy marshes and decaying trailer parks the train was swaying past.

He was fretting over the results of last night's fourth floor exploit. What did he really know? That Vollmer was part of some *Rote Königin* operation. Check. What did he suspect? That Vollmer was a hacker, working in concert with accomplices unknown. Check. What was the purpose of said hack? Stealing money. Check. And what, finally, did he not know? That any of his observations and suspicions meant anything at all. Fuck.

At the Hamilton Station he remounted his bike and pedaled slowly along the path to the New Horizons Enterprise Center, lost in thought.

Halfway there he came to a wooden bridge over a narrow creek still trickling in the heat of a Northern California summer. The creek banks on either side of the path had been landscaped to form a small park. Wooden benches were in position to offer a relaxed view of the local wildlife.

Page turned aside, propped his bike against one end of a bench, and took a seat. His arrival alarmed a snowy egret that exploded out of the reeds and flew twenty yards before settling down to resume foraging for its breakfast.

He opened his Timbuk2 bag and withdrew his laptop, preparing for an open-air psych session with his chatbot, when a nearby voice startled him:

"Tire flat? Need some air?"

It was the red-haired woman in the lime green helmet, who had apparently caught a later train. She was standing astride her bike and pointing at his.

Page was taken aback. "Oh, my bike? No, tires are fine. I'm just having a think. You know . . . thinking."

"Trouble at work?"

"Nahh. Um, bird watching. I just spotted an egret. We don't have those where I come from."

"And where is that?"

"Chicago," he confessed.

"Yeah, who would live there?"

"Not me, obviously. Cheaper, though."

"Careful with the thinking," said the red-haired woman with a smile. "It's dangerous, can lead to ideas."

She eased back onto her saddle, kicked at the path to get rolling, and zoomed away.

"Have a nice day," Page called out to her diminishing form. She waved without looking back.

Page cast an eye around to be damn sure no one else was nearby, then opened his laptop and launched Master Ming.

"All right, Doc, little help here — I know I shouldn't ask, should decide on my own like a big boy, but I'm lost — what about this red queen stuff? Should I talk to the authorities?"

Ming made no response for a long second, causing Page to fear that his virtual mentor had been waylaid by a bug. But then the answer swam into view:

CAST ASIDE ALL DOUBT

The imaginary seer's advice, contrived by Page months ago to boost his self-confidence, was finally on view to boost it. How about that! He hauled out his smartphone, dialed 411 to find a telephone number, got it, and dialed the Novato Police Department. A soporific female voice answered on the third ring and led him through a long list of choices to the desk sergeant of the day.

"Imhoff here. What's your problem?"

"Uhh, hello, good morning," stammered Page. "I've got a situation at my company. A guy who works here is . . . uhh . . . *hacking* into someone's bank accounts."

"That doesn't sound good. Your company — is it located within Novato city limits?"

"Yeah, it is."

"All right then, we're interested. Company name? Your name?"

Page hesitated, suddenly worried about getting himself into a lot of trouble.

"Oh boy, should I tell you? I've never done anything like this before."

"You don't sound too sure of yourself."

"I'm not."

"Okay, then, here's a suggestion — go to our website and file a report online. Either that or, if you are a whistleblower and disclosing your name might place your job in jeopardy, there's a button you can click on and leave an anonymous tip."

"Unh-huh, I should probably do that."

"Make sure you have some evidence. Our department aggressively prosecutes anyone who files a false report."

"This is real. No doubt. I think a lot of money might be at stake, but I don't know everything yet."

The desk sergeant seemed to register Page's actual honesty under the evasive manner. He thought for a moment.

"Tell you what — there's another way to do this. Contact the feds. They're the ones who we'd call anyway, were we convinced of a case. We don't investigate this stuff ourselves."

"Unh-huh. The feds. Which ones?"

"Oh, I don't know . . . NSA, CIA, anyone in the snoop group."

"NSA?"

"No Such Agency."

"Ahh, the National Security Agency, duh. The spymasters."

"Right. This is their territory, I think."

"Okay, thanks."

▼

Later that day while DuFrayne was out on her lunch break, Page dialed a mysterious telephone number he had tracked down online. A robot receptionist answered. She boldly announced that Page had reached the National Security Agency and offered several cryptic call routing options. Page tried them all, but none ended up reaching a living, breathing, talking human being.

"Crap," he said and put away his phone.

At first he was annoyed by the call failure, but after brooding on the problem for a while he found his mood unexpectedly brightening. He had done as much as could be expected of any upstanding citizen, he told himself, and he was relieved that his suspicions weren't going to drag him into any unforeseen personal crisis.

35

00100011

Two days later a new label came through the Arrowshaft ship-ping department printer that troubled DuFrayne. A collection of *Combo Warriors* Devil Heads, Terror Torsos, and Flying Feet was wanted in California at a very odd address.

"Did you see this?" She waved the label in front of Page's nose. "I know you're into this crazy stuff."

Crazy indeed:

```
Red Queen Studio
P.O. Box AE FE 27 99 D9 F9 23 76
La Honda  CA  94020-0011
```

They packed and sealed the game pieces without further specu-lation, but Page hesitated to put the box in the mail.

"Where's La Honda?" he wondered, initiating a computer search on Google Maps.

"Down on the peninsula," replied DuFrayne.

"The peninsula?" Page had never once crossed the Golden Gate Bridge since his arrival in California. His idea of local geography was sketchy at best.

"South of San Francisco somewhere," said DuFrayne airily. "High-tech hippies live there. At least, that's what I've heard. I've never actually seen the place."

Page examined an online map and found the obscure little town located on the mountainous spine of the South Bay peninsula, a few miles toward the coast from Palo Alto and Stanford University.

"I'll deliver this thing myself," he declared.

DuFrayne looked at him cross-eyed.

Like many companies in the knowledge worker trade, Arrow-shaft had a policy allowing any employee to claim one *personal day* a year in addition to whatever vacation time he or she had coming.

The human resource policy was designed to accommodate unexpected emergencies.

Page considered that the oddly-addressed package represented just such an emergency. Not only that, it gave him an opportunity to call Brava Erpenstock, who technically oversaw his shipping operation.

"Brava? Oliver."

"Who?"

Page winced when his name was not instantly recognized.

"Oh, Page, it's you," said Erpenstock, recovering quickly. "Sorry, I'm distracted today. Lots going on up here."

"Oh right, I know you're busy."

"Very. How are things down there in Fulfillment?"

"Um, fine, good, going well. We're a well-oiled machine down here."

"That's a relief. One less thing to worry about."

"Yeah, we're on top of things. The reason I'm calling is because I need to take my personal day tomorrow."

"Of course. Your privilege. I'll make a note. Thanks for letting me know."

After he put down the phone, he ruminated on the conversation. Naïve as he was, infatuated as he was with the marketing goddess, he nevertheless was starting to develop some of the same cynicism he noticed in himself while toiling at Brass Knuckles.

"Hey, Duffy, get this — our supervisor actually referred to our little shop as *Fulfillment.*"

DuFrayne shook her head. "I feel our work is very fulfilling, don't you?"

They both laughed.

▼

Early next morning Page set out for La Honda, with the suspect package on the passenger seat of his car.

Crossing over the legendary Golden Gate Bridge filled him with awe and drove home a sobering realization. Even though he had hardly met anybody since moving west, he was never going back to Chicago, except, he silently promised himself, on a brief visit someday to check on Gram.

When he arrived at the San Francisco end of the bridge, the toll gates were unmanned, and he rolled right through without slowing down. He marveled over the slick software that enabled an invisible camera to photograph his license plate, extract a home address, and send him a bill.

The drive took an hour and a half, much of it in slow-and-go commuter traffic. San Francisco itself, Highway 101, and the streets around Palo Alto were dense with the results of the fevered business boom in Northern California's high-tech industries. He had never seen so many Audis and Mercedes and Porsches and Teslas on the road.

While he was creeping along he considered his abysmal social situation. He had managed to alienate his only friends, or at least put them on their guard. His acerbic co-worker's oblique but obvious attentions made him uncomfortable. At the same time, he had to admit that, of all the women he had ever met, she was the only one he actually enjoyed talking to. If only he could shake off his fixation on Brava Erpenstock.

"My mind is a mess," he said aloud. "Get over that woman." But his psyche rebelled, and his heart continued to beat faster whenever he gave Erpenstock a single second's thought.

La Honda was nestled among steep hills on narrow winding California Route 84. The post office was hard to spot. After cruising through the heavily forested village twice, he found it in a long wood frame building that also housed a real estate company and a non-profit help center for people down on their luck.

Inside, no one was on hand to serve any customers. Page placed his shipping box on the counter and rang the call bell. After what seemed like forever, a scruffy young man emerged from the sorting room, clad in a sleeveless knit shirt. His hair was long on one side and shaved on the other. His fingernails were painted black.

Page took a backward step.

"Yes? What can I do for you, sir?" said the young man.

Page pushed his box forward.

"Hi, there. I've got this package to deliver. I'm a shipping clerk up the road a ways, and I can't figure out the details."

He pointed to the label and its strange P.O. box.

"See? That's a funny box number, am I right?"

The young man stared at the label. He dragged a finger along the hexadecimal digits.

"I guess so. Never seen one like it until a few weeks ago."

"You've seen others for Red Queen? New to me."

"Yeah, well, the numbers change, but we're briefed, we deliver, don't worry about it."

"How's that work?" queried Page.

"We forward all the mail to an address in Palo Alto, *no problemo.*"

Page noted an evasive vibe coming off the young man, who didn't look like he had been on the job too long. He decided to push his luck.

"Someone pays you to forward these things, right?"

The young man's pale white face turned even whiter.

"I've got these labels they gave us." He held up a pad of printed addresses and flipped through the sheets to demonstrate. "I just slap 'em on the parcels, and away they go. Simple forwarding, nothing wrong with that."

"Not at all," agreed Page with a sympathetic nod. "Sometimes I run into the same problem." He glanced around the spare interior. "Say, I don't see any priority mail boxes on display. I need about six of them. The big ones. Got any handy? Be a big favor if you do."

The young man raised a finger. "Hang on a sec, I'll check."

He placed the pad he was holding on a shelf under the counter and disappeared into the sorting room. As soon as he was out of sight, Page reached over the counter, grabbed the pad, and peeled off the top label.

One minute later he was driving back north. He noted the address on the gummy slip of paper he had commandeered:

```
Red Queen Studio
421 Manzanita Street
East Palo Alto  CA  94303
```

▼

That evening Page met with his indie team at Puerto Seguro. He was very nervous about getting together after his moralistic explosion during the last meetup.

"James . . ."

If Fillmore harbored resentment, it didn't show. He was quick to perform a cordial high-five.

"We're cool, dude."

Karen Hoffman gave him a big hug and a kiss on the cheek.

"Hi, Ollie. Good news, I've got the final sound assets. Music, effects, everything."

Page raised his eyebrows.

"Bought and paid for with my own credit card," said Fillmore defensively.

"And we need you to install them into Unity," added Hoffman.

Page felt his tension evaporate. "Okay, that's easy. I'll text over the nomenclature and you can hook 'em up from there."

Fillmore nodded approval, emboldening Page to talk about a different problem.

"Meanwhile, guys, I need to figure out how to piggyback on someone's Wi-Fi. It's password protected. How do I do it?"

Fillmore shrugged. "Why ask me?"

"Because you're the only hacker I know."

Fillmore dipped his head in a little bow. "And you, Mr. Clean, want to cheat your internet provider? I'm speechless."

Page's cheeks turned red.

"It's embarrassing . . ."

"Can't afford Comcast's prices, huh? Got a neighbor who streams Netflix?"

Page was about to correct this impression, then thought better of the idea.

"That's it. Netflix. Save a few dollars."

"Well, well, well," smirked Fillmore.

"So, what's my move?"

"Start by getting yourself a copy of Kali Linux. It crunches passwords like breakfast cereal. It's available right there in the Windows 10 store. You can run it from a USB drive."

"Kali Linux. Sounds spooky."

"Oh, it is, it is."

36
00100100

Page spent the next day downloading Kali Linux and experimenting to be sure he could run it from a USB thumb drive as promised. Once he had the basics under control he spent hours poring over online articles about password hacking. He could barely understand any of the lore, but he did learn how to run the network cracking program called *Rooter* that came with his copy of the mysterious operating system.

"What are you up to now?" asked DuFrayne, tired and sweaty from wrangling big boxes in the company shipping bay.

"Software project. No big deal," said Page, hoping to deflect attention.

"Ooh, that sounds like a lot more fun than moving the junk we sell. Need any help?"

Page looked up from his computer screen. DuFrayne took a step closer.

"How are you with computers?" he asked.

"Terrible," she said.

Page closed up his laptop.

"So the answer is, no, no help needed. How about you? Devil Heads? *Pony* crap?"

DuFrayne's posture sagged.

"Big order from Malaysia just came in. We could sort the stuff."

Page nodded, donned work gloves, and together they put away all the toys and trinkets and T-shirts on their proper shelves in the warehouse.

At the end of the day, Page made no effort to leave. The mission he was preparing for seemed to demand night work. DuFrayne hung around as well. Was she waiting for an invitation of some kind? He considered his own reactions whenever he was confronted with Brava Erpenstock's total indifference, and those painful thoughts generated sympathetic feelings for his co-worker. He warned himself not to confuse sympathy with affection.

When he was convinced the rush hour was over, he grabbed his laptop and headed for the exit.

"Hey, wait up."

DuFrayne was hurrying after him.

"Got your car today?"

"As it happens . . ."

"Mine's in the shop. Bum a ride?"

Page groaned. Busted, on the one day he didn't ride his bike.

"Sure thing. Where to?"

"Toyota dealer. It's just up the road."

They joined the evening traffic flow on the freeway heading north toward Petaluma, and Page turned into the Toyota lot just past the Vintage Oaks shopping center.

"Here you go, have a nice evening."

DuFrayne opened the car door, but didn't step out.

"Thanks for the lift. Um, if you're hungry, there's a really good Chinese restaurant just around the corner."

Page froze.

"Oh, gosh, I've got a long evening ahead. No can do."

"Hmm, too bad. What's so important you can't grab a bite?"

"Well, it's . . . heh-heh . . . espionage."

A light bulb went on over DuFrayne's head.

"Oh-ho! The latest crazy address we got, down on the peninsula."

"Yeah, I'm going to check it out. Get to the bottom of this."

"Can I come too?"

DuFrayne locked eyes on Page, whose self-confidence shriveled away under her warm gaze.

"Look," he said. "It's a nice offer. Dinner, too. But whoa . . . bad idea . . . this is going to be a commando operation."

DuFrayne's manner abruptly cooled.

"You? A commando?" she sneered icily.

Page bobbed his head. "Yup, that's me. Your one-man gang."

DuFrayne slid out of the car with a dismissive wave and slammed the door.

▼

With the help of Google Maps, Page made it through San Francisco and down the peninsula to 421 Manzanita Street in East Palo Alto in just over an hour. He cruised past the house, which was a rundown stucco-clad duplex. On one side, the windows were dark. A *FOR SALE* sign stood at the curb. On the other, lights blazed on both floors. Rubbish and recycling bins were tipped against a small porch. An older VW Jetta was parked in the drive. A BMW motorcycle was parked on the lawn beside it, along with a pile of spare tires, an Adirondack resort chair, and oddly, a discarded toilet, on whose lid someone had scrawled *FREE* with a felt tip marker.

Although new to the West Coast, Page had quickly acquired a Californian's appraising eye, and he judged that the seedy property could not be worth less than $750,000. What a bargain.

He circled around the block and cruised by again to absorb the layout of the house and yard, then drove three blocks away and parked on Lincoln Avenue.

He put on a San Francisco Giants baseball cap, pocketed a small digital camera, took his laptop in hand, and marched back to Manzanita, attempting to look casual and feeling very exposed.

At the house itself he eased around the darkened half into the back yard. The only sounds of habitation came from a heavy metal rock band on a stereo system inside. He couldn't identify the tune.

A fire pit bordered with concrete blocks had been dug in the middle of the yard. Beer cans littered the scraggly lawn all around it.

Page deliberately kicked one. If his presence was going to set a guard dog barking, he wanted to be forewarned. But there was no reaction.

"Okay . . ." he breathed.

He inserted the Kali Linux thumb drive into his laptop and pushed the power switch.

Within a few seconds he was inspecting a list of Wi-Fi networks running in the neighborhood. Which one belonged to his target? The strongest signal came from *Netgear (1),* followed by *Netgear (2),* followed by *Polly Wolly.* Nestled below them, still showing five bars, was something called *RQS.*

"Red Queen Studio?" he speculated aloud. "Gotcha!"

He launched the Rooter program. When the query to name a Wi-Fi network appeared, he typed in *R-Q-S.*

In response, the program warned him that the network was protected by a security system. A query appeared with choices. Page wasn't sure, but selected WPA2.

Next, the program queried for a password.

"Password?" he muttered. "Good God, if I had the password I wouldn't need you . . ."

Instead, he clicked on a button labeled *Find Password.* Online documentation had warned him that Rooter might take as long as an hour to crack a protected network password, but optimistically suggested that the usual time was less than half that. Page was ready to wait. He sat down on a concrete block and watched while a little set of dots cycled around and around to show that Rooter was working on the problem.

To pass the time, Page rehearsed his plan of action. When he finally penetrated the Red Queen network, he intended to search through each of the hackers' computers for an incriminating folder name. He would be looking for something like *hacks* or *bank accounts* or *money trees,* but if that didn't work he would file the network password, disconnect, and drive home. A more general attack would have to wait for another night.

But Page didn't have to wait thirty minutes for results. Two minutes and thirty seconds after Rooter started prying into the RQS network, he heard shouts and curses coming from the house. A moment later the back door banged open and a large man emerged on the steps.

"Hey! What the fuck is going on out here?"

Page was jolted by the unexpected turn of events. He was discovered! The hackers had somehow spotted his probe. His limbs jerked spasmodically, and he barely avoided wetting his pants. He snapped his laptop closed and leaped to his feet. The large man hefted what looked like a vacuum cleaner hose and rushed toward him, swinging the attached wand like a baseball bat.

Page skipped aside just as his assailant closed within a short step. He heard the vacuum wand whistle by his head as he dodged away and ran for the far corner of the house, moving, with the aid of a powerful surge of adrenaline, as fast as he ever had in his young life.

Pelting onto the front lawn, he almost tripped over the tires piled there. The large man was right behind him.

"Hör auf, du Fickkopf!" he yelled in German.

Then the front door slammed open, and another man came running. Page zigzagged past them both and continued on around the house and into the back yard again, juggling his computer as he ran. He could hear his pursuers panting and cursing as they followed on his heels.

Out of the corner of his eye Page noticed an old bicycle leaning against the house as he dashed past. He redoubled his efforts and ran around the house once again, gaining a few yards on his pursuers with each stride. Too many hours sitting in front of computers left them gasping and wheezing.

On this lap he snagged the bike and ran it into the duplex's paved driveway. There he leaped into the saddle and, cranking hard, accelerated away from 421 Manzanita Street.

He had gone a block when he heard the roar of a motorcycle engine, followed by the shriek of tires burning rubber.

"Oh my God, I'm dead."

Three houses further up the street he saw a hedge around someone's yard. He squealed to a stop, threw the bike over the hedge, and crouched down behind it, hugging his laptop. Seconds later the motorcycle roared past.

Page waited in hiding for several minutes, a terrifying period that seemed eternal. Eventually the sound of the motorcycle faded away. Still he hesitated, acutely aware that two different men were after him, and one might be stalking him on foot.

But no footsteps could be heard. He stood up to walk away, and was actually out on the sidewalk when he heard the motorcycle returning. This time it was moving slowly, hunting. He dove back over the hedge and flattened himself on the grass behind it as the motorcycle rolled by.

"Komm raus, kleine Maus, we won't hurt you!" warbled the rider.

Page waited another five minutes. Soon, as the adrenaline wore off, he was shivering.

Suddenly a porch light came on, and a woman leaned out of an open doorway.

"Who's there? Get away, you homeless bums!"

Page crawled to the side of the woman's house, stood up and dove over the hedge again. This time he tumbled into a neighboring side yard. Without waiting for further challenges, he hopped the decorative fence enclosing the property and legged it down the street to the Lincoln intersection.

There was his car, half a block away. He hobbled along the avenue favoring a hamstring strained by his hedge tactics, unlocked the

Honda with shaky fingers, and fell inside. A moment later the motorcycle rounded a corner into view. Page locked the driver's door and ducked down as low as possible.

The motorcycle passed by without stopping to inspect the aging automobile.

Page waited for a few seconds to allow his heart to slow down, then started the car and drove the hell out of East Palo Alto.

He was rolling over the Golden Gate Bridge before his head cleared enough for him to evaluate the evening's adventure. He was safe. Hooray for that. But he failed to penetrate the Red Queen Wi-Fi network and obtain the slightest shred of evidence concerning the group's nefarious activities . . . if any.

Damn.

▼

When Page finally stumbled into the Petaluma garage he called home, he lifted a beer from his tiny refrigerator, popped the cap, and paced the tiny living space in circles, thinking hard. He was sure the angry hackers who chased him were up to no good, whether he had any actual evidence or not.

He swigged his beer, removed the clumps of muddy grass stuck to his laptop, and sat down to compose a long email message.

37
00100101

Warren Ash was driving his classic 1967 Mini Cooper back to
Baltimore after a weekend rally in Williamsburg, Virginia, running
third in a line of seven other Minis, when his phone buzzed

He checked the number. Uh-oh, something important at work.
The radically engineered but antique auto dated from well before
its driver was born, and certainly before hands-free Bluetooth ac-
cessories were available, so Ash risked a distracted driver fine to
answer the call. What he heard made him veer away from the rest
of the Minis, and drive directly to the National Security Agency's
Friendship Annex.

There he revved up his computer to check on the latest attempts
to penetrate the Folsom Dam gate controls. But there was nothing
new on his screen. He was becoming convinced that the threat was
a hoax intended to extort money. Unless something solid turned up
soon, he would issue a report to that effect.

The call that pulled him into his little cubicle was robotically ini-
tiated by the Air Traffic Control software package he used to monitor the work of hackers, and he did not understand what triggered
the alert. He scanned through the list of pings recorded during the
last several hours to get some perspective. Among several hundred
items, the only one that stood out was a peculiar message in plain
text from an I.P. address associated with Arrowshaft Interactive
Media and connected, apparently, to the ongoing Rabobank probes
he was occasionally watching.

He opened the message on a second screen. This is what he saw:

* Terror * Covert * Dirty Bomb * Conspiracy * ISIS
* Kill * Blow Up * Assassinate * Steal * Detonate
* Agent * Iran * Semtex * RDX * Fertilizer Bomb

* Nitroglycerine * Terminate President * Zap Congress
* Occupy Capital * Ransom * Neo-Nazi * Commies

Hey, NSA —
Did the above trigger words get your attention? I hope so. I tried to call, but your telephone tree ran me ragged.

I have knowledge of hackers operating from inside my company. What are they up to? Your guess is as good as mine, but whatever it is, it can't be legal.

The group calls itself Rote Königin Median in Germany and Red Queen Studio here in the US of A. Under the guise of developing financial software, I believe they are looking to make a bank heist.

Maybe they want to get rich, or maybe they want to finance a terror squad.

No doubt this message will reveal all my personal details. Don't bother checking, here's everything you need to know:

Name = Oliver Page
Social Security Number = x2335
Company = Arrowshaft Interactive Media
MAC address = 00:90:96:65:D6:5F
IP address = 67.169.42.51

Give me a call, would you, please?

Ash was stunned by the extraordinary communication and impressed by the bold method used to aim it in his direction. He checked to see if any of the IP addresses he was looking at in connection with the Rabobank probes tallied with the sender's list. They did. Well, what do you know? Might be a breakthrough.

▼

At Arrowshaft, Page returned from the company kitchenette with pre-fab lattes just in time to receive a mysterious phone call. DuFrayne was standing at the department desk holding out the handset with a puzzled look on her face.

"Who is it?"

"Spook city, boss," she said.

He exchanged a cup of coffee for the phone.

"This is Page."

"Oliver Page?" came a man's baritone voice.

"That's me. Who is this?"

"I can't really discuss it. Social ending in 2335?"

"Yeah . . ."

"I received a message today that might have come from you. Sound familiar?"

"I'm no terrorist, if that's what you're thinking."

"No comment. What makes you think you have a hacker onboard out there in California?"

"This is the NSA, right? You work for them."

"Don't worry about me. Let's talk about your discovery. What's the scoop?"

"I work in the shipping department here. We call it Fulfillment. I have noticed weird details on some of the labels we print. All addressed to Red Queen something or other in Germany."

"How so weird?" The voice was skeptical.

"P.O. boxes with sixteen digits in hexadecimal notation. Crazy, but not if they are part of some kind of code, right?"

"Sixteen digits? We'd crack that code in five minutes."

"Sixteen hex equals sixty-four binary digits. I'm guessing my hacker is sending out a one-time pad, randomly generated with a Mersenne Twister algorithm, like the one I use on a chatbot I invented."

"Still too simple."

"Right, but then salted with some reference to the Red Queen in that book, *Through the Looking-Glass.*"

"Alice?"

"Her second big adventure."

"Here's what I want you to do. Use the same trigger words as a message header and send me a copy of every screwy address label you've ever slapped on a package."

"Then what?"

"Forget you ever heard my voice."

▼

Back East in the Friendship Annex, Ash and his boss discussed the turn of events.

"One-time pad?" scoffed Ufford. "No self-respecting air-gapping SHA-coding hacker broheim would dare."

Ash wasn't so sure.

"Our walk-in informer thinks they salt the numbers with some reference in Lewis Carroll. The Red Queen, whoever she is."

"She's a chess piece that comes to life. Don't tell me you never read the classics."

"Whatever. The labels we're talking about are all addressed to *Rote Königin* or Red Queen. Could be an index of some kind."

Ufford scowled.

"How much for the Nutcracker to squeeze hard?"

"The Mouse King says two-hundred-K. That's for running the numbers we see on twenty-seven labels backwards to grab the seed. Going to take fucking forever."

"The Russians did it to Vegas slots. We could too, but I'm not going to spend that kind of money."

"Come on, Sandy, the money is just nominal. Let's ride."

"For what? Save a Dutch bank? We'd be laughed out of the company."

38
00100110

Page's preoccupation with the Red Queen and secret hacker codes was unexpectedly overshadowed by a job opportunity.

The August all-hands meeting of Arrowshaft employees in the second-floor multi-purpose room was devoted to Doyle Magowan's stout defense of the company's business trajectory. He forecast a *PieceMakers* hit, and a ship date before Christmas, with profits to roll in during the next fiscal year. Ben Seabury then stepped forward to outline the company's swing toward financial services. He offered details of the new banking app under development and held forth the rosy vision of steady revenue in the near future. Arrowshaft, he declared, was about to free itself from depending on hit video games to make money.

Not everyone in the audience believed what they heard, including Page. In fact, the more enthusiastic the pitch, the more doubtful he became. He left the meeting in a pensive mood and bumped right into Vivian Romero on his way out the door. The collision wasn't an accident.

"Ollie, how are you? Got a minute?"

"Oh, hi, Viv."

He used first names now that he was, like all of his fellow employees, a cynical company veteran.

"What's up in HR?"

"Nice you should ask. We're looking to hire another programmer. I'll post the opening, and we may have to go through the interview motions . . ."

Page remembered his previous rejection with some bitterness. "I understand, gotta be fair."

". . . but the job's yours if you want it."

Page was thunderstruck. A programming job. Finally.

"Really? What about the store?"

"Our sales volume has dropped somewhat. Emilee can handle it on her own."

"Well, this is, um, good news, I guess, right? Um, terrific actually, um, well . . . *yes!*"

"Come see me and we'll talk details. You'll start right away."

"PieceMakers?"

"Or the new banking app. We need to get it out the door, and Karsten is way stressed."

"Oh sure, whatever, I'm up for it."

"Good. Schedule is tight, but we don't plan to throw you under the deadline bus. You won't be our only new face in development."

Romero patted Page on the shoulder and strolled away, leaving the young shipping clerk in a euphoric daze.

Over lunch he texted his grandmother:

Hey, Gram —

Just got my break @ AIM. Going to be a programmer now, like I hoped. This is big.

xoxo — OP

Page then called Fillmore with the news.

"Jimmy? Arrowshaft is looking for programmers. I'm moving upstairs, and you could join me."

Fillmore was not excited.

"Forget it, Ollie. I'm happy where I am."

"I didn't know you were independently wealthy."

"I'm not. Just independent."

"You sure? This is a real good opportunity."

"Very sure. I don't need an Arrowshaft in the back, thanks."

"Don't be so negative, things are looking up over here."

"Looking up is different than being up, bro."

▼

Page brought DuFrayne a latte from the Butterfly to ease the difficulty of explaining his good fortune and the unpleasant facts of her new workload.

"Know what, Duff? You should be running the shop."

"Damn right. But instead, I work for you."

"Theoretically. We're more like a team, I'd say."

"Some team."

Page sipped his coffee, plotting a course through DuFrayne's various temper triggers. He reached into a paper bag.

"Here, I brought you a raspberry croissant."

She accepted the pastry with a little frown.

"Okay, wise guy, what's going on? You're never this nice."

Page grimaced.

"Looks like you're taking over here."

"What?"

"It's a promotion."

"Oh really? And you . . ?"

"I'm going to be a programmer. Upstairs in development. I just found out."

"Who's going to help me lift boxes, pray tell?"

Page twisted his lips into a wry smile. He ran a nervous hand through his hair. "No one. You're on your own for a while."

"That is so fucked."

"I know. Totally."

39
00100111

In going through the latest bin of incoming fan mail, invoices, and sales orders, DuFrayne came across a padded envelope addressed to her co-worker in a funny way:

Detective Page

She rode the elevator upstairs to personally deliver the item to the junior programmer who was just settling into a cozy spot in the middle of cubeland.

"Ollie . . ?"

Page was arranging his new desk.

"Duffy, check this out — tomorrow is my first day, but I get to launch my new career ahead of time."

"Lucky you. Meanwhile, look what just showed up in the mail downstairs . . ."

She handed over the padded envelope. Page frowned at the *Detective* prefix on his name and tore off the envelope's perforated tab, whereupon a small thumb drive fell out.

"Huh, what's this . . ?"

He looked to thank DuFrayne for the mysterious gift, but she was already walking away.

"Love your cube," she said. She didn't glance back.

Page examined the drive. White plastic, made by Sony. 32GB. He tossed it back and forth from hand to hand. What the hey?

Two hours later his mobile phone rang.

"Got the drive I sent you?" came a baritone voice.

"Got someone's drive, anyway. How did you know?"

"Don't fuck around with that thing, it's dangerous."

"Who is this?"

"My name's not important. We talked before."

"Mmm . . ."

"You told me you had a hacker there at Arrow-something."

"That's right, we do."

"I want you to insert that thumb drive into one of the USB slots on the hacker's computer. While it's running, natch."

"Uh-oh, he's right here in this room, like four cubes over. I can't go near there until he leaves. And what if he shuts down his machine? I don't have his password."

"You won't need it. *Harvester* will sniff around on its own."

"*Harvester* — ? You're kidding."

"We never kid anyone. Leave the drive inserted for thirty minutes. No less. Then pull it."

"How do I know it's doing . . . whatever it's doing?"

"You don't know anything. It's better that way."

▼

Page prepared himself for yet another late-night venture into off-limits territory by making a dinner out of potato chips and Mountain Dew from the kitchenette snack machines. Then he pretended to study up on the company's version control system, its accepted programming styles (no cuddling allowed), and the *Money Matters 360* codebase in the Unity development system. He was hoping to find some incriminating lines in Vollmer's files, but all he learned was that the ace programmer knew less about the software engine they were using to power their financial app than he himself did. Something to remember when he actually got going on the project.

Soon the sun dropped behind the western hills. Soon after that twilight started to fade. Soon after that he saw Vollmer lever himself out of his chair and depart for the evening.

Page waited for quite a while before he dared to approach the man's cubicle.

Vollmer's machine was running its lurid screensaver when Page bent to insert the mysterious thumb drive into a USB slot in the PC under Vollmer's desk. As soon as he did, the screensaver stalled and *Zutritt Verboten* appeared in its place.

Page returned to his own desk, noted the time, and sat back to let whatever was going to happen, happen.

Thirty minutes later he returned to Vollmer's desk and removed the device.

Thirty minutes after that his smartphone rang.

"Page here."

"We're in. We're confused," announced the anonymous voice on the other end of the call.

"Wow, you're working late."

"Sleep is for civilians. *Harvester* has found a Mersenne Twister program on the machine you tapped, but it doesn't generate the keys to the codes we see. And the unique hardware MAC address is different. In fact, it looks like *your* hardware address."

"Oh shit. He's spoofing my identity."

"Or the hacker is actually you."

A little chill ran up Page's spine, even though the idea was preposterous. But wait, what about that meetup at the Butterfly when Fillmore got into his machine . . ?

"Me? Then why would I write to you guys?"

"Criminals are weird, and cyber criminals are practically extraterrestrial. You never know."

Page was desperate to deflect suspicion and couldn't stop himself from blurting out the ideas that were festering in his head.

"Look, you want keys? You need to account for the Red Queen stuff."

"We think that's just a distraction."

"Oh yeah? Try looking at *Through the Looking-Glass* for the first mention of the words, *Red Queen*. Then use the zip on each label — they're all different — to count from that point forward and modify the crazy P.O. box number with whatever word you land on. Do that, perform a hash, and bingo — now you've got an unbreakable one-time pad."

"Jesus, keys from a book. Just like the quaint old days in World War One."

"Extraterrestrial thought patterns, right? Here's another possibility — maybe the hackers are using the zips to indicate previous labels — there are quite a few — and they stir the P.O. box numbers from those labels into the mix — make their new code with help from some of the older ones."

"Very imaginative, detective."

Page was annoyed by the patronizing tone.

"Okay, how about this? The labels are just the *salt* and some long passage in *Alice* marked by a Red Queen reference, — when hashed, right? — that's the real code. That key could be any length. Any length at all."

"Mmm."

"Turn your supercomputer loose. *Through the Looking-Glass* — it's Red Queen this or Red Queen that. Gotta be."

"Unless it's not."

"Want another tip?" offered Page, clocking the doubts. "Buy yourselves a copy of the German translation."

"German translation . . . now, there's a thought."

40
00101000

Page spent little time worrying about the NSA or whoever was calling him at all hours.

Next morning, he yanked his bike from an early SMART train at the Hamilton stop and rode toward work with his head in the clouds.

As occasionally happened, the red-haired woman in the lime green helmet was on the same train, and she was biking swiftly toward the same destination. Page was happily anticipating the coveted new job that awaited him, and his mood was playful.

"Race you!" he shouted and dug into his pedals.

The red-haired woman appeared to ignore the challenge. Page watched her drop far behind in his rearview mirror. He congratulated himself on the surprise move.

But then she accelerated. They rattled over the wooden bridge marking the little trailside park side by side. In another moment she was a hundred yards ahead, then a quarter of a mile. She waved. Soon she was out of sight.

"Whoa, babe, too fast . . ."

Page was exhausted by his sprint and slowed to a more leisurely pace. Thoughts of his new job kept him from brooding over the small athletic defeat.

In the office he sprang into the elevator with Unity commands dancing in his head. He already had a better idea for allocating financial assets in the company's money app than Herr Vollmer.

Page stepped out of the car on the fourth floor eager to get his fingers on a keyboard. And there he was met by Vivian Romero. The HR manager was wearing a long face. She pressed a hand against his chest to bring him to a halt.

"Bad news, Ollie."

"Beg pardon?"

"The job I promised has been canceled."

Page was flabbergasted. "What . . ?"

"The company is going through a rough patch. Restructuring. Well, not really, but we're trimming here and there."

Page sobered up in an instant. His brow creased with suspicion. "What's going on, Viv? Pardon me, but what the fuck?"

Romero looked down at her shoes.

"It's not up to me, Ollie. Our owners, Almaden Capital? They're laying down the law. It's a survival move."

"Survival . . ."

"When we ship, the situation will improve."

"How? How will we ship if I don't roll up my sleeves?"

"Until then, it's back to Fulfillment. I'm truly sorry."

Page realized he was overflowing with hot liquid rage.

"This company is effing effed!" he boiled.

"Don't say it!" warned Romero, losing some of her sympathetic warmth. "Could be worse, you know. We could have laid you off."

Romero's hint at small favors jolted Page like a lightning strike.

"Oh my God . . ." he said and turned back into the elevator.

▼

Emilee DuFrayne was packing her things when Page ran into the department to find her.

"They stick it to you?"

She swiped at her cheeks, smearing angry tears. She gave Page a sullen nod. "I'm out of here."

"Oh God, I'm so sorry."

"Not your fault," she sniffled. "How about you?"

"My programming gig evaporated. I'll be down here again."

"And I'll be out on the street."

Page nodded in turn. Losing a job was no fun, and in the modern economy, always a life-changing threat.

"Look, with your ability, your, uh . . . dedication . . . you'll find something easy."

"It's never easy, Page. Even a golden boy like you knows that."

Page chewed his lip. He had not the faintest idea how to counsel or console his co-worker.

"I hear stuff." He shrugged self-consciously. "Maybe I'll get a lead. Call me."

"Yeah, you know I will."

They stared at each other in silence. Then DuFrayne stepped forward and enveloped Page in a tight hug.

It lasted three seconds. Then she backed away and was out the door, suddenly jaunty, swinging her bag full of office things.

Page watched her go in dismal confusion.

>>> 0101
PART FIVE

41
00101001

The following week's work was a bone-and-spirit-crushing night-mare. A dozen large shipments came in, another hundred smaller ones went out. Page's tape-gun arm was so sore he could hardly raise it above his head.

Worse, during the infrequent idle hours his thoughts turned to DuFrayne, and he realized, with nagging pain, that he missed his laid-off colleague. Missed her easy face. Missed her careless hair styles, missed her grimy T-shirts, missed her unpredictably acid tongue.

After a few days he tried to call her. She did not pick up, although there was a voicemail greeting:

"Hi, it's almost me, Emilee. Leave a message, and if I like what I hear, maybe I'll call you back."

Page smiled at the tone.

"Hey, Duff. How ya doin'? Got a job yet? Call me."

But she did not respond. For a week he called every day, just to hear the sound of her recorded voice and the sour attitude that went with it.

▼

Most of the time Page was too busy to brood. His mind was seething with details of inventory, invoices, and shipping manifests when a call from an anonymous person in the surveillance trade interrupted his rhythm.

"Afternoon, Mr. Page."

"Uhh, morning out west, sir," he replied.

The voice, although mysteriously redolent of secret agencies, was not the voice he had previously dealt with. Page called the owner *sir* for no good reason, except that the man behind it sounded calmer and more mature than his last contact.

"Morning, afternoon, dark of night, it's all the same to us, Oliver . . . ahh . . . may I call you Oliver?"

"Call me whatever you want. How could I object?"

"Well, you can't, I suppose. Let me get to the point, Oliver. Thanks to your initiative, we now have a tag on your hacker pals."

"Oh good, that's good."

"Yes, very. We also found out what they're doing, and that's not so good."

"Of course not. I mean, how could it be?"

"They're stealing money from your company and your parent company."

"Uh-oh."

"Uh-oh indeed. The sums are large."

"Are we in trouble here? Financially?"

"Probably. Let me ask — does the hacker you tapped, the man named Vollmer — does he have access to your financial controls?"

"Well, he's working on a financial app for smartphones. Convenience for people on the go who need to deposit checks, pay bills. All in a little three-dimensional town. It's pretty radical."

Page thought for a moment, remembering the *Money Matters 360* files he had been studying.

"But, no," he concluded. "he can't get his hands on stuff like our IBAN or SWIFT info, let alone burrow into an account that's not his."

"That's interesting, Oliver. I'll tell you why: your hacker is most certainly burrowing into your accounts. Know what that means?"

"Sorry, no . . ."

"It means he has an *accomplice.*"

Page's blood ran cold. Oh my God, that night upstairs, when Brava Erpenstock was rummaging around in the financial office, what was she up to?

"Gee, sir, this is terrible news. What do you want me to do?"

"Uncover the accomplice, if possible. That is" — here the voice chuckled ironically — "unless you yourself are that person."

Page recoiled at hearing his innocence questioned . . . again.

"The other guy who called me — agent, analyst, whatever the hell — works for you, right? He wondered about me too, but I'm not a thief . . . sir."

"No, probably not. Get us a name. Someone trusted who is abusing that trust. Once we have all our suspicious ducks lined up, friends of ours will make a move."

"Make a move?"

"Agents will act."

"Unh-huh. Got it."

Page was feeling damp under his armpits.

"Problem is, sir, there's not much I can do. I work down here in the warehouse."

"Give it a try, we think you're very resourceful."

"Do my best, sir."

▼

Page was addled by the surreal conversation. He was worried that hackers were sinking Arrowshaft. He was also worried that Brava Erpenstock was going to be arrested for embezzlement.

Neither thought was comforting, so he hauled out his chatbot to help him decide what to do.

His first step was to prime the random number seed on his laptop computer with a radioactive signal from the makeshift Geiger counter he had constructed. Then he pointed the laptop camera at a variety of colorful shapes. After that he attached a light sensor and aimed his LED-flashing Galaxy Spinner at the thing.

Once he had established what he thought of as the basis for a truly random number, he appealed to his chatbot:

"Hello, Master — I've got a big problem. I've uncovered a nest of hackers bleeding the company, and I'm in love — I guess that's what you'd call it — with the person who, I'm pretty sure, handed over the keys to the bank vault. Some dilemma, huh?"

Ming blinked. He made a noncommittal humming sound.

"Yeah, I'm a dweeb talking to you. Gotta get over it, but this is important. I need your help."

Ming's eyebrows wiggled.

"So, in the form of an actual question — what should I do? Give the feds her name? Or, no, no, wait, maybe she's innocent. Here's the real question — should I warn her?"

Page counted to nine and pressed the spacebar.

The mandarin's advice faded in below his unsmiling face:

PUT AWAY CHILDISH THINGS

Page was startled by the answer. His chest constricted, and his head started whirling like his Galaxy Spinner. His superstitious revision of a chatbot advisory had showed up to haunt him at the precise moment it would have the very impact one part of his psyche desired and another part hoped to avoid.

Brava Erpenstock was in her office laying out an advertising plan for *PieceMakers* when Page knocked.

"Hi, Ollie, what's going on downstairs?" She spread her hands over the papers scattered across her desk. "As you can see, I'm awfully busy."

Page didn't wait for an invitation. He strode purposely forward, hauled a chair around the side of her desk and sat down.

"Yes? You look worried." She shook a loose strand of golden hair into place.

Now that he was face to face with his idol, the courage he had been working up on the elevator slithered away.

"Um . . . yeah, I am. Worried . . ."

Erpenstock sensed something rolling around inside the awkward shipping clerk.

"What's bothering you? Our schedule? Don't worry, we'll make it, we'll be fine. Ben Seabury is finalizing a company re-org that will save us months of work. *PieceMakers* is a sure thing. We'll sell millions of units. And our move into finance is going to be a big success."

Hearing the fair one trot out a shameless version of standard corporate boilerplate worked to harden Page's resolve. He felt himself recovering, gathering strength, felt an icy coolness overtake his usual dithering manner in front of her.

"Brava, you're in trouble. We're all in trouble."

Erpenstock's cheeks turned red. The idea of being challenged by an underling . . .

"I beg your pardon!"

"I don't know any of the details, but the cat is out of the bag."

"What cat? What bag? What are you talking about?"

Page swallowed hard.

"Oh God . . . you gave that fat jerk Vollmer the passwords to our bank accounts."

"I did what — ??? *Never!*"

"He's using them. He's draining money out of our company."

Erpenstock's lips curled.

"Where, you little turd, did you ever hear something like that?"

Page didn't like being called a turd. His eyebrows knotted. He glowered involuntarily.

"Try the NSA."

"Who?

"The National Security Agency. The feds."

"Oh for Christ's sake! You? The feds? That's rich!"

Page stood up. He tilted his head sympathetically.

"They want a name from me. If they push hard enough, threaten me or something, I'll have to give it to them."

Erpenstock leaped out of her chair, scattering the plans for her advertising campaign. Her eyes were blazing.

"Like hell you will."

Even when burning with hideous fury, Page couldn't help noticing how beautiful she was.

"Listen to me, Brava. I know what's going on. I've been tracking the Red Queen for months. It's over. This is a warning."

"Aren't you nice? The newbie turdlet deigns to hand his supervisor a warning."

"You should take it as a favor, that's how I mean it."

Erpenstock laughed bitterly. She made a little curtsy.

"Fine. A favor. Now get the fuck out of my sight!"

Page held up his hands to declare a truce and backed out into the hallway.

42
00101010

Vivian Romero called an impromptu all-hands meeting to discuss unexpected changes at Arrowshaft Interactive Media.

"Good morning, all. Thanks for showing up on short notice. I have some announcements. First off, I very much regret to tell you that Brava Erpenstock, our marketing manager, has resigned her post, effective immediately."

Gasps and groans issued from the assembled employees.

"We all know that Brava is an ace, and we will feel her loss. She has always been passionate about optimal advertising, and an opportunity has recently come her way that was just too good to pass up. She's leaving us to join a startup, High Beam Consulting, as their executive vice president."

More groans and moans.

"We wish her well. Ben Seabury, our chief financial officer, will take over Brava's duties in the near term."

Whispering gossip blew through the group like a winter wind.

"There's more," continued Romero. "Karsten Vollmer, the lead programmer and conceptual originator of *Money Matters 360*, will be leaving the company as well to pursue other interests."

Another round of gripes and grumbles.

"Now hang on, people, I've got good news too. *Pony Corral 9*, our latest mobile title, has hit *Golden Master*. That's a big milestone, and with that out of the way, Vitus Lozoraitis will take over the lead on *Money Matters*. Leo Thorpe, our principal designer, has agreed to fall back on his programming skills and help get *PieceMakers* out the door."

Romero looked out over her audience. The faces were frowning. No one seemed very enthusiastic about any of her news, good or bad.

"What's the latest timeline, Ms. Romero?" shouted someone from the back of the room. "Got a schedule for us?"

Romero waved airily.

"I don't have dates. But both products will be out there for Christmas."

She held up her hands to forestall any further questions.

"That's it for today, folks. Back to work. Christmas isn't that far away."

▼

Only Oliver Page knew the real reasons for the changes described by Romero, and he wasn't inclined to talk about them. Even he didn't know that Erpenstock's new company was nothing more than a checking account that she desperately hoped to leverage into a genuine advertising company.

The announcements, coming out of the blue as they did, set off another gossip explosion and another frantic round of resumé revisions. Page observed the turmoil with detached amusement. Deep inside he knew his days at Arrowshaft were numbered. He just didn't know the number.

Now and then his thoughts turned to the ex-marketing beauty. Images of her perfect face, golden hair, and sexy curves occasionally danced through his brain whether he willed them (as he sometimes did) or not. They gradually took on a bitter cast.

He was proud that Erpenstock had acted on his warning after all. He had the secure knowledge of rendering her a small service, the single consequential event in their entire relationship. But, whoa, some relationship, dude, he reminded himself. He was no knight in shining armor practicing courtly love, and she was nobody's fair lady. He was beginning to understand that he never registered as the faintest blip on her personal radar. The knowledge filled him with terrible shame.

He would have found it hard to sleep at night, but he was getting little sleep in any case, because the indie mobile game *Aggrozoid Defenders* that he was developing with Hoffman and Fillmore was nearing completion, and coding up the details was taking every spare hour of his time.

43
00101011

After many an all-nighter hammering out the complexities of a modern mobile game, the holy grail of *Beta* status was drawing within reach of the three *Aggrozoid* developers.

They exchanged phone calls. They tentatively congratulated each other. All that was required to reach the penultimate milestone was a joint session of the three co-creators to merge their code and assets.

"Puerto Seguro, seven o'clock," ordered Hoffman.

Page agreed, even though he knew that some of his code was still shaky.

"How shaky?" asked Hoffman, suddenly worried.

"Not too bad. I want to clean up my random number generator. It works, but when I run it, I see a pattern."

"Fix it over dinner," advised Hoffman.

"Okay, see you then."

▼

At the restaurant, the team was in a carefree mood. They ordered margaritas. Their hard work, all done in spare time and stolen hours, was near to paying off.

All three hooked their laptops to the eatery's public Wi-Fi network, and Page collected their work onto his machine. He then compiled their files — containing reams of code, hundreds of art assets and dozens of sound effects — into a playable version of *Aggrozoids*.

"Are we there?" he wondered hopefully.

Hoffman revved up her smartphone and started the game in her special developmental sandbox. They took turns watching the little monsters scuttle across the dining room floor to attack their makers.

After their enchiladas arrived, after their second margaritas were polished off and their third ones ordered, Fillmore opened up a window on his laptop.

"Show you something, kids . . ."

He tapped some keys and turned the computer around for Page and Hoffman to see.

"Jesus, Jimmy." Page was horrified. "An ad for our game. Is this online?"

"You bet it is."

"How many sites?"

"Fifteen, I think. They'll run through release."

"You pay for them?"

"Not really. In case you didn't notice, we don't have a Kickstarter campaign. No venture capitalists hovering around us all excited, showering down coin."

"And you promised." Page shook an accusing finger at his unruly teammate. "This is fraud. Fraud or theft or something. We talked about it. I thought we agreed."

Hoffman shrank back in her chair and busied herself with her rice and beans.

Fillmore shrugged indifferently. "Remember that song? Oops, I did it again? We need the ink, Ollie. The project comes first. It always comes first. You know that as well as I do."

"Honesty comes in there somewhere."

"Well, I didn't just hack ourselves onto the gaming pages. Money changed hands. The ads are legit."

"What money? What hands?"

"Some company rolling in dough made an involuntary contribution to help support the indie movement."

"That is so lame. You're using money that doesn't belong to us. You stole it!" Page was outraged.

"We're small. We need to stick our asses out there, get noticed, sell units, my friend, or it's all over. You want to give up?"

"There's got to be an honest way."

Fillmore turned to Hoffman with an ironic scowl on his face. "Listen to this guy," he scoffed.

What they were debating was a new advertisement for *Aggrozoids* that Fillmore had placed on more than a dozen gaming sites. Advertisements created, judging from the sophisticated graphics, with Hoffman's artistic touch:

GET THE AGGROZOIDS
BEFORE THEY GET YOU!
Defend your mobile device!
Available for Android & iOS just in time

Suddenly the website open on Fillmore's computer, left to sit idly while the threesome wrangled, vanished. A colorful screensaver flashed into view in its place. Fillmore was quick to notice. He turned the computer away from Page and pressed a key to reinstate his advertisement.

It all happened in the blink of an eye. But Page formed the impression that he had briefly glimpsed the picture of a chess piece among the churning screensaver images. A red queen, no less.

Page choked back an outcry. His skin felt numb. A tangle of dark thoughts knotted his brain. He sucked in air and exhaled slowly.

"Look, Jimmy, I don't want to fight about this. You're right, we need the spotlight. It's important. I get it."

He raised his glass and drank off the rest of his third margarita.

"Here's to discovery."

Hoffman leaned over and kissed him on the cheek. Fillmore stuck out a fist. Page bumped it.

"No hard feelings."

"None."

His colleagues were ready to pack it in for the night, but Page had other ideas.

"Whoa, almost forgot. I promised Karen I'd fix up my random number generator. Get rid of the pattern in there."

Fillmore was dubious. "Who else would ever see it?"

"Don't know. *I* see it."

Fillmore groaned. "You down with this, Karen?"

"Yes. Supposedly we're at *Beta.* I want an honest *Beta.* "

"My girl the producer. How long will it take?"

"Not long." Page pointed at his head. "I've got a plan. Order some fried ice cream. Ten minutes, tops."

Three scoops of fried ice cream arrived. While they all picked at the exotic confection, Page deliberately wrote a bug into his random number code.

By the time the ice cream was gone and the check for dinner was on their table, Page had rigged the game to generate a zero and crash any time a pair of sixes showed up in the long number that governed how the aggrozoid swarm did its swarming. He figured that the bug would show up every couple of thousand times the function was called. After five or ten minutes of playtime, say. Often enough to get noticed, but not right away.

Once the code was integrated into their latest build, they all said good night and left the restaurant. Page alone, heading for his cramped garage, Fillmore and Hoffman hand in hand, obviously planning a night together.

"We're at *Beta,* you guys!" called Page cheerily, sounding tipsy.

They waved.

▼

In the NSA's Friendship Annex, Warren Ash called Alexander Ufford over to his desk the moment Air Traffic Control picked up the transmission.

"Hey, Sandy, another message in a bottle just washed up on my screen. You gotta see it."

Ufford made the long walk around and between the dozens of cubicles separating his office from Ash's corner outpost.

"What have I got to see?"

"This . . ."

> * Terror * Covert * Dirty Bomb * Conspiracy * ISIS
> * Kill * Blow Up * Assassinate * Steal * Detonate
> * Agent * Iran * Semtex * RDX * Fertilizer Bomb
> * Nitroglycerine * Terminate President * Zap Congress
> * Occupy Capital * Ransom * Neo-Nazi * Commies
>
> Hello again, NSA —
> Red Queen update: Got another hacker suspect. What should I do?

Ash scratched his head.

"Our boy out west. How do you want to handle this?"

Ufford drummed his fingers on Ash's desk.

"What time is it out there?"

Ash looked at his watch.

"Nine-thirty."

"I'll make the call."

▼

Page was in the Arrowshaft shipping department, overwhelmed by product-boxing duties, when his smartphone rang.

"This is Page."

"Hello, Oliver. How are you this morning?"

For a second, Page thought he was getting some damn robocall, but then he realized it was the older of the pair of spooks who had reached out to him.

"I'm okay, sir. You saw my note, I guess, huh?"

"We see many things."

"I'll bet. But probably not the latest red queen stuff."

"Another hacker?"

"I think so."

"Name?"

"Not ready for that. What if I'm wrong?"

"Good for you, Oliver — protect the innocent. Admirable trait, considering that our investigations sometimes go wrong. Too bad we can't deduce everything like Sherlock Holmes."

"You said it. Then I wouldn't have to get involved."

"If wishes were horses . . . still got that thumb drive?"

"I do."

"Well then, you have the perfect means to identify a dangerous criminal actor and establish your own innocence."

Page registered the implied suspicion, and he stiffened inwardly under the heavy pressure.

"My innocence? Whoa there, I'm not involved. Not in any way."

"And you can prove it, Oliver. Use that thumb drive to copy *Harvester* onto your suspect's computer. We'll take it from there."

▼

Page fretted over the idea of turning Fillmore in. They were on the same team. They shared goals. Yet it had to be said, Jimmy crossed the line. Not once, but three times at least. Those ads for *Aggrozoids* he made with stolen money after promising to stop. The secret connection he forged with the Red Queen conspiracy. Worst of all, it now appeared that he stole the hardware address of Page's laptop to throw suspicion onto his trusting pal. The last item was going to cause trouble, and it was nothing less than a callous betrayal of their friendship. Page puffed out a sad sigh. Whose money was floating through Fillmore's hands, he wondered. Arrowshaft's? Probably.

On the other hand, the spooky types didn't care who got hurt. Sure, their words were smooth, full of sympathy, but that was all posture, nothing but a load of government bullshit.

Weighing big decisions filled Page with anxiety, so he did what he always did — he flipped open his laptop and pressed a key to consult good old Ming.

In a few seconds the chatbot was running, and Page's virtual counselor was gazing enigmatically out of the computer screen at his actual acolyte.

"Hey there . . ."

Page started to speak, then lapsed into a long silence, several fevered thoughts away from a decisive question.

"What am I doing?" he asked himself finally. "I am pathetic."

Another long and tortured silence. Then . . .

"I saw what I saw. I know what I know."

Page reached out and closed the lid of his laptop, shutting the door on Master Ming, and severing his reliance on the wizard's random advice.

Then he opened up the Unity software development system and spent some time repairing the bug he had inserted into the *Aggrozoid* program. After that he revised his random number generator to remove the repetitive pattern of monster attacks he had spotted.

When his copy of the game was running smoothly, he added the NSA's *Harvester* spyware into the codebase.

▼

Soon thereafter his smartphone rang again. Karen Hoffman was on the line, and she was mighty annoyed.

"Hey, Ollie, what the heck is going on with your so-called *Beta* code?"

"What are you talking about?"

"There's a horrendous A-bug in there."

"Can't be me."

"It sure is. Three minutes after I start playing, all the little aggrozoidies disappear and our game just dies. The monster code is yours."

"Oh boy. I'll take a look. When I smoothed out that pattern I was looking at, I may have screwed up something else."

"How long to fix?"

"Not sure, but I'll get on it."

"Make it quick, I'm coming over there."

The call ended, and Page had to smile. His improvised tactic to stop the Red Queen hackers was actually working.

Since his *Aggrozoids* repair work was already complete, he was busy packing and shipping when Hoffman arrived.

"This is where they keep you?" she asked, looking around at all the boxes and the workaday industrial décor. "Unless you failed to fix that bug, it's a big waste of talent."

Page grinned.

"Bug is fixed. Open up your laptop, I'll send everything over."

Hoffman positioned her computer on the department work-bench. Page signed her into the company Wi-Fi network and cop-ied his latest computer code, together with the *Harvester* surveillance program, onto her machine.

"Thanks, Ollie."

Hoffman playfully tousled his hair.

"You need to get out of here. You know that, right?"

Page shrugged.

"Anyway," she continued in full producer mode, "here's the plan. I've got to clean up a few of the screen graphics, compress them down, spiff up the logo. Meet us at Puerto on Wednesday night. Week from now. We'll combine everything then."

"I'm ready."

She punched him on the arm.

"Golden Master — we're almost there, dude!"

44
00101100

Page got to wondering about the fate of Karsten Vollmer and the German men who chased him around East Palo Alto. Every morning he studied the local newspapers online: the *Independent-Journal* in Marin, the *San Francisco Chronicle* in The City, and the *Mercury News* down on the peninsula, looking for any items about hacking and possible arrests. He found none.

The more he thought about it, the more curious he became about the cause of Vollmer's sudden departure. How much did management know about the man's activities? How did they find out?

▼

The answer to Page's questions were privately discussed at a meeting between the executives of Arrowshaft Interactive Media and Almaden Capital Management at One Embarcadero Center in The City.

Over a cordial lunch of crab cakes and chardonnay, meant to calm and disarm his visitors, Albert Weisbrod was briefing Doyle Magowan and Ben Seabury over a cyber attack Almaden's back office employees had recently discovered.

"To give you the full picture, Arrowshaft's main operating account has lost something like eight hundred and fifty thousand dollars in the last two months. That's a fairly good-sized chunk of cash, wouldn't you say? Why did you not notice? Care to explain, Mr. Seabury?"

Seabury squirmed in his chair.

"Somehow, one of our programmers got into our accounts. Ours and yours, apparently. He was able to disguise the transfer orders, keep them off my radar screen. However, as soon as we were notified by your people, we terminated the man."

"Yes, our horses are gone, but the barn door is now closed, and legal action may follow. An indictment, hopefully."

"Hopefully."

Weisbrod rattled a fork on his plate.

"You have to understand, gentlemen, that this was not an unauthorized penetration via some weakness in our security."

"No? How is that possible?"

"The thief had help. He discovered our account numbers, passwords, authentication keys, everything. He was collaborating, apparently, with fellow hackers down on the peninsula and in Germany. The money involved has vanished into secret offshore accounts."

Seabury glanced at Magowan.

"Bad hire, bad apple. It happens."

Weisbrod gritted his teeth. He sipped his wine.

"Luckily, an alert was passed down from a federal surveillance team. But damage has been done. I cannot divulge the exact totals, but your hacker managed to steal a lot more from us, from Almaden itself, than from you. Rabobank has been informed. They are redoubling their security measures. Now disclosures have to be tactfully composed, explain the problem to our clients without scaring their investments away. Mr. Nazari and Mr. Karnovsky find the situation . . . embarrassing."

"Of course they do. This is terrible."

Weisbrod bit into a crab cake.

"It calls into question the viability of Arrowshaft. I hope you two are prepared to ship product and recognize substantial revenues in the very near future."

Magowan drew a breath. "It's software development. It never happens overnight, as I'm sure you know. We're targeting Christmas."

Seabury leaned forward. "We've juggled our teams for maximum efficiency. Shoppers will have our financial app on their phones by Thanksgiving, ready to spend in a whole new creative way. This is going to be big."

"I await results," summarized Weisbrod, forcing a smile.

▼

On the way back to Marin County, Magowan restlessly drummed his fingers on the steering wheel of his Tesla.

"How much did Almaden lose, you think?"

Seabury was slumped down in his chair, staring at the brown hills rolling by the car.

"I peeked at the reserve account they keep for us. Vollmer's pals hollowed it out. There was more than a million in there three months ago."

"Holy shit."

"Shit is right. We are in deep."

"You know, Ben, I've always had an urge to try my hand at a more speculative trade. How about you?"

"I never think too far ahead. You can lose a lot of sleep that way."

45
00101101

Warren Ash was shutting down his surveillance operation for the evening when a new message from the West Coast arrived. He showed it to Alexander Ufford. Ufford sat down in Ash's office chair and spun himself around three times. He leaned back and stared at the ceiling. He opened up a package of Wrigley's spearmint gum and chewed thoughtfully.

"Call our enforcement friends?" suggested Ash, arching his eyebrows into a behavioral question mark.

Ufford didn't answer right away. Eventually he placed his hands on his knees and rose slowly to his feet. He tapped the screen where the message was on view.

"Get back to you."

▼

Page executed three preliminary builds of *Aggrozoid Defenders* and played each one on his smartphone for an hour, preparing for the final version. The tiny team couldn't afford actual testers, and he wanted to be damn sure no accidental bugs remained in his code before he joined Fillmore and Hoffman for the ritual finishing touches.

As discussed, he arrived at Puerto Seguro right at six-thirty and parked his Honda across the lot from the restaurant. A nondescript Ford Taurus was standing nearby. Page failed to notice the middle-aged driver whisper into a walkie-talkie as he strolled past.

Inside, Fillmore was already holding down a seat, and Hoffman showed up a few minutes later.

"Traffic is hell," she explained.

Fillmore ordered fish tacos. Hoffman chose flautas, and Page stuck with his go-to Mexican dish, chili rellenos. They shared a tall pitcher of house margaritas. Blended, no salt.

The threesome fired up their laptops and collected their files on Page's machine over Wi-Fi. He then executed a new and, barring some unexpected malfunction in the Unity engine, final build of the game, secretly free of the NSA's *Harvester* spybot.

The build took a few minutes to complete, even on Page's elite laptop with multiple processor cores firing away at three-point-nine-five gigahertz.

When the computer code files, the graphic assets, and the sound effects were all baked together, Page sent the results back to his teammates.

They knocked back their margaritas in a toast to video games in general and their precious creation in particular.

"To the indie life!" said Hoffman. She then downloaded the mobile Android app onto her Samsung phone and began to play. Fillmore and Page showed each other their crossed fingers, both of them laughing at their superstitious anxiety. After ten minutes Hoffman had destroyed a horde of skittering little aliens with nary a glitch.

Fillmore's turn. He copied the iOS version onto his Apple iPhone. After ten minutes he had consigned wave after wave of cute little zombies to zombie hell.

"We're clean," he announced.

High fives and fist bumps all around. Glasses refilled and drained again.

Hoffman lifted sheets of paper from her backpack.

"Okay, boys. Now we sign our blood oaths."

She handed out a boilerplate contract with blanks filled in to indicate joint *Aggrozoid Defenders* ownership, legal names and addresses, rights of audit, et cetera et cetera. They each signed five copies and sealed the deal with yet another round of margaritas.

Page then copied the game itself and all its parts onto a microSD card the size of a fingernail. He pushed the tiny sliver of plastic across the table in Hoffman's direction.

"What's this?" she queried, picking it up.

"Put it in your pocket," he advised. "Backup . . . just in case."

"In case of what?"

"You never know, right?" The evening was warm, and moisture had appeared on his brow.

Fillmore peered at his friend. "You okay, Ollie?"

Page nodded.

"No more tequila for you, pal." added Hoffman.

Page nodded again.

She signaled the waiter and ordered flan for all and strong coffee for Page.

▼

Outside in the shopping center parking lot, two Chevrolet SUVs, big black ones, circled the rows of customers' cars and parked on either side of the Puerto Seguro entrance. Three men and two women emerged. Heads of passersby in T-shirts and tank tops swiveled toward them, because the five were all dressed in dark suits, paying no respect to the late summer heat.

Inside, Page looked up as the five suits entered and fanned out, moving slowly toward the *Aggrozoid* table.

"I just want to say, you guys, that working with you has been the best experience of my life."

"Oh, Ollie, that's so sweet . . ."

A moment later the five suits were standing in front of the trio. Hoffman and Fillmore looked puzzled. Page shrank down in his chair.

"Oliver Page? James Fillmore?" inquired one of the women.

Page raised a hand. "Here," he said.

Fillmore sat back in his chair with his arms folded over his laptop.

"Who are you?" he demanded, even though it was obvious they

were law enforcement agents.

One of the agents, an older man, stepped forward, opened a wallet, and showed off his badge.

"Agent Barnes. FBI."

Fillmore flipped open his laptop and jammed his fingers down on the keys. Agent Barnes leaned forward and grabbed the computer away.

"I'll take that, son," he said and launched into a litany of federal criminal complaints. "You, James Fillmore, and you, Oliver Page, are under arrest for computer fraud, first for accessing protected computers across state lines with intent to defraud for financial gain, and second, for intent to cause damage to government infrastructure in the form of the Folsom Dam in Sacramento."

Hoffman was in shock. She noticed the painful guilt written on Page's face.

"Oh my God, Ollie — you did this. You brought these people down on our heads!" Tears sprang into her eyes.

One of the women took possession of Hoffman's computer. Page, gloomily resigned to the future contempt of his teammates, voluntarily offered up his own laptop.

Fillmore was enraged by his friend's betrayal. "You, you shit! You are totally fucked, man!"

Page gave his head a miserable shake. He pointed a finger.

"You crossed the line, Jimmy," he said in a shaky voice. "More than once. You said you wouldn't, and then you did. Red Queen, sound familiar?"

Fillmore lunged at Page, but was restrained by two of the agents.

"And why are the feds coming after me?" continued Page. "You're the only one who's been inside my laptop. Vollmer was spoofing my MAC address to look like me. And he could disguise himself because you stole my junk and gave it to that creep."

Fillmore's angry expression softened. He began to relax. He scratched his head. He cracked a crooked smile. "Sold it," he said.

"Pardon me?"

"I don't give stuff away. I sold it."

Hoffman endeavored to clap a hand over Fillmore's mouth.

"Jesus, Jimmy."

Fillmore dodged away.

"And that's all I ever did. Sell stuff."

Agent Barnes thrust out his arms to cut off the angry debate.

"Let's continue our discussion somewhere more private, shall we?"

The other agents rousted the threesome and snapped nickel-plated handcuffs on Fillmore and Page.

Hoffman held out her own wrists.

"You can go, Miss," said one of the women.

Hoffman stamped a foot. "Fuck you, I'm with him," she said, clutching a fistful of Fillmore's shirt.

"No you're not, Miss. Be grateful we can't prove you're involved. Now step aside and go your merry way before we take you in for obstructing a law enforcement agent in the performance of her duty."

"Get out of here, Karen. Go, git!" implored Fillmore.

"I want my computer back," she huffed.

"In due course. But for now, it's evidence."

One of the junior agents leaned toward Hoffman. "Word to the wise, Miss . . . rip yourself a new one. These cases take years."

Hoffman glared at the man and stomped out the door.

▼

"You have the right to remain silent. Anything you say can and will be used against you in a court of law. You have the right to an attorney. If you cannot afford an attorney, one will be appointed to you by the court."

The FBI and their prisoners were holed up in separate rooms in the Embassy Pavilion Hotel in San Rafael. Agent Wigan, one of the younger men, was reading the Miranda warning from a card.

"With these rights in mind, are you still willing to talk with me about the charges against you?"

Oliver Page was sitting on one of the king-size beds in the room. His hands were still cuffed.

"Yeah, why not? I'm the guy who tipped whoever tipped you."

"Sure you did," responded Agent Wigan. He punched a button on a digital voice recorder to turn it on.

"Red Queen. A guy working in my company," insisted Page.

"What company is that?"

"Arrowshaft Interactive Media. We make video games."

Agent Wigan was amused. He turned toward his partner. "Hey, Simone, you hear that — they make video games!"

He refocused flinty eyes on Page. His grin vanished. "And you — you've been playing *Monopoly* with your company's money. Stealing it, right?"

"Whoa, there, Sherlock. May I call you Sherlock?"

Agent Wigan's face reddened. "Don't be a wise-ass, kid. When the hammer comes down on your toe it will sting."

"Sorry. You're making a lot of assumptions here. I don't know anything about the Red Queen's activities, and I tried very hard to find out. I know — roughly — how they encrypted their communications, but I didn't actually crack their scheme wide open."

Agent Wigan was not impressed.

"Now, before you continue with your lies and evasions, be aware that we have the built-in hardware ID of your computer — the exact same computer used to transfer all the money involved."

"You have a MAC address. It was given — sold, he now claims — to your actual criminals by a guy I thought was my friend."

"So you claim."

"Yes I do . . . I do so claim."

The other agent in the room, a woman in her forties, stepped forward and placed a hand on her partner's shoulder to signal her turn at bat.

"Mr. Page. First, let me identify myself — Simone Harney. I'm a special agent, which means I can effect an arrest, put you away. So please talk sensibly and truthfully to me. Agreed?"

Page gave the woman a sullen bob of the head.

"Oh good, we have an understanding. I'm curious about your account of the situation we have uncovered. Spoofed a *hardware* address? That's a pretty good trick, wouldn't you say?"

Page shrugged. "I couldn't do it."

Agent Harney nodded. "Let's put all that aside for a moment. You have mentioned something called the Red Queen several times. Explain."

"It's a group. They communicate by cooking up an encryption key they can post on a shipping label as a P.O. box, and then exchange encrypted messages using it. But then after a few transmissions, they switch to another code using the same basic ideas."

"A one-time pad, I believe that's called. Am I right?"

Page nodded. "Yes, ma'am. And the term Red Queen? It's an index point in *Through the Looking-Glass.*"

"Beg pardon?"

"I see other numbers that mean something on the shipping labels that go through my department."

"What department is that?"

"Shipping. Well, officially it's called Fulfillment."

Agent Harney smiled. "A name to conjure with."

Page rolled his eyes.

"Those extra numbers — phony zip codes, say — tell the bad guys to look past a reference to the Red Queen in Lewis Carroll's book, combine the next couple of hundred words they find with the crazy P.O. box address, and hash it all. That gives them the key to the latest batch of secret messages. Without that key, the code is unbreakable."

Agent Harney blinked. "Whoa, that flew right over my hairdo."

Page inclined his head toward the voice recorder. "You can catch it on the replay."

"Yes, I will. Who concocted this unbreakable code, this encryption scheme, whatever? You?"

"Not me. But I think it might have been my clever friend, who knows a lot of stuff he never told me about."

In a room down the hall, Agent Barnes was conducting the FBI's interrogation of Jimmy Fillmore, also cuffed, also sitting on a hotel room bed.

"Let me warn you, we have traffic between your computer and several members of the so-called Red Queen gang, both here and in Germany. We know you're involved."

Fillmore was in a peculiarly jaunty mood.

"Bet you haven't decoded anything yet."

"I have no personal knowledge of progress on that front. But be assured, we have friends who will get to the bottom of this."

"Maybe, if they work hard enough. It's like mining for bitcoin, takes a big helping of computer oomph."

Agent Barnes steepled his fingers to suggest mild displeasure.

"You seem awfully calm and confident for a man facing the prospect of several years in prison."

Fillmore grimaced. "No disrespect meant. I'm aware of the danger."

"In that case, I'd like you to tell me, tell my little voice recorder here, all about your threats to force open the gates of Folsom Dam."

"What?"

"A ransom was proposed. How would you have done the deed?"

"Oh for God's sake. I'm not involved in any of that Red Queen crap. Not the German stuff, and especially not the splinter group here in California. Those guys are crazy."

"There's a group in Germany?"

"In Hannover."

"Names, please?"

Fillmore recoiled. "I don't have any names. I sell encryption services, and I do it on the dark web. No one knows any *names,* dad."

"And the California group?"

Fillmore hesitated.

"You know, I did hear a rumor that those bozos would try to extort a lot of dough from the water guys. It's funny."

"What's funny about internet blackmail?"

"Well — I don't think Folsom Dam actually has any controls subject to online sabotage. And the Red Queen guys didn't think the operators knew enough about their own system to be sure."

Agent Barnes groaned. "Probably not," he said.

"Did the hoax work?" wondered Fillmore.

"I don't know. Moving on — let's talk about your collaborator inside Arrowshaft."

"Karsten Vollmer. What a slimeball."

"No, no, Oliver Page. The young man cooling his heels next door with my colleagues. You were in this together. Maybe he made it look like Vollmer was the hacker. Maybe he wrote the code you were all using. Maybe you're just a pawn in his game. What do you say?"

Fillmore was insulted by the insinuation.

"Page? He could never create a decent coding scheme. He's an okay programmer, pretty solid actually, but he's no hacker. He's completely innocent."

"Oh really . . ."

"Forget about Page. I'm the unbreakable code guy."

Agent Barnes made a face.

"You sound kind of proud of your fraudulent activities."

Fillmore grinned mischievously.

"Oh, I am. Very proud. And I should be, I'm good at what I do."

Perhaps you'd like to discuss the details. I'm all ears."

"With all respect, Mr. Barnes, you wouldn't understand a thing I might say."

"Try me."

"I'd much rather try someone who works for the NSA."

▼

Agent Harney interrupted her probing chat with Page to take a call on her mobile phone. It lasted less than a minute. When it was over she crossed the room and removed the handcuffs binding him.

"Get up," she commanded.

Page slid off the bed and stood up.

"What's going on?" he inquired. He was confused. Agent Harney didn't bother to answer. She stationed herself at the hotel room door.

There came a loud knock. Agent Harney swung the door open and Agent Barnes entered, looking grave. He strode across the room, reached out for Page's right hand, and clasped it tightly.

"Seems like we owe you an apology, Mr. Page. Apparently we have you to thank for spotting the Red Queen operation and breaking it wide open."

"It's broken?"

"Arrests are being made, here and in Germany. And you, sir, are free to go."

"What about my friend Fillmore?"

"That's a different matter. He's under arrest. Fraud charges, money laundering, we'll work up a good list."

"No way. You heard him, he's just a shady businessman."

"And you are one lucky guy. He cleared you."

"He did what?"

"He doesn't think you'd ever be much of a hacker, but he had to admit you figured out his scheme, when no one else, including our secret agency friends, had a clue. He's proud of you."

Page was dumbfounded by the accolade.

"Will he go to prison?"

"If he goes to trial, if he's convicted, if the judge has any sense . . . yes he will."

Page hung his head in shame.

The FBI man's face clouded sympathetically. "As for you, get out of here. Just don't leave the country. You may have to testify."

▼

Page trudged out of the hotel in a daze. There at the curb was Hoffman, leaning against the passenger door of her car, apparently waiting for Fillmore.

"Hey, Karen, I know you hate me, but I'm not sure a lonely vigil is a great idea right now. They've arrested Jimmy."

Hoffman barged forward and slammed a fist into Page's stomach, doubling him over.

"Unnnhh . . ." he moaned.

"There, you bastard. I know all about Jimmy, some guy came out to tell me. I was waiting for you."

"Urfghh . . ." said Page.

"Get in, I'll drive you to your car."

"What's the idea? I turned him in."

"Yeah, you're a self-righteous shithead, But the microSD card you made with the *Aggrozoid Golden Master* on there? It's going to save our indie butts."

46
00101110

Twenty stories up in the Embarcadero One office building, high above San Francisco Bay, Albert Weisbrod was briefing his superiors, Maksim Karnovsky and Samir Nazari, who had just returned from a deal-making trip to Tokyo, on the situation at Arrowshaft Interactive Media.

"On the prophet's tomb, if we wanted such risk, such volatility, we could have invested in Tesla," growled Nazari, when he learned of the game company's delays and financial setbacks.

Karnovsky shifted in his chair.

"I understand the hacker group — what did they call themselves? *Krasnaya Koroleva?* — have been eliminated."

Weisbrod allowed himself a wry smile. "There have been several arrests."

How much money did the hackers take out of Arrowshaft?"

"Just under a million."

"And our accounts?"

"About one million two."

"I want our money back!" snapped Nazari.

Weisbrod held up his hands in a stop gesture. "Take it easy, Sammy. We won't get it."

"And why not?"

"Switzerland. The Cayman Islands. Panama. It escaped. Now it's going to finance the hackers' legal eagles."

"Blood, then!" roared Nazari. "I have to write apology to our investors over this, so must be blood!"

Karnovsky gently placed a hand on Nazari's arm to calm him.

"Tell us, Alyosha, how Arrowshaft is doing, when the losses will stop."

Weisbrod rose from his comfortable chair and stood at the tall picture window. He spent a moment gazing thoughtfully at container ships plowing the waters under the Bay Bridge.

"Their latest video game — successor to a big hit, remember — has been derailed by management incompetence. The financial application for phones and tablets will, if brought to completion, sell a few hundred units to various banks, but not any, really, to the general public."

"Go on," urged Nazari.

Weisbrod sighed. "There is no hope of recovery unless we babysit them with tens of millions of our own capital."

Karnovsky snorted. "And take a hands-on position in management."

"That too, Max."

"Your advice, counselor . . ." prodded Nazari.

Weisbrod's lips curled into a thoughtful twist. He waved a hand suggestively.

"Think of the attractions of a tax write-off. We will do better shielding other income with an Arrowshaft bankruptcy than we ever would by propping the company up."

"You mean close doors," said Karnovsky, to be sure he heard correctly.

Weisbrod nodded.

Karnovsky stood up and paced the length and breadth of the conference room.

"Okay. But we have eggs on our head from this hacker business, and now this. So . . . must be orderly. Everything orderly."

47
00101111

Vivian Romero was beside herself. Out of the blue the Arrow-shaft vice president for human resources was facing another management crisis and the grim prospect of staging another demoralizing all-hands meeting on short notice. Yet she was a pro. Twenty years of corporate life had taught her patience and forbearance. Her long experience (plus a little nip of vodka from the stash under her desk) was all she needed to step up and earn her pay.

At the appointed hour, she strode through the gathered employees and took a position behind the lectern in the second-floor meeting room. She was aware of subdued gripes and grumbles coming from the attendees. She recognized the hum of discontent.

"Good morning, everybody."

Dead silence.

Romero looked over the group, smiled, and pushed a pair of stylish glasses up onto her forehead.

"I have some announcements on this beautiful fall morning. Ready for some important news?"

A wave of yeas and nays rumbled through the room. Romero gauged the prevailing sentiment to be on the negative side. That put her in a reckless mood.

"First, I have to report that Doyle Magowan, our fearless leader, and Ben Seabury, our chief financial officer, have both tendered their resignations, effective today."

Groans and nervous laughter erupted.

"I know, I know, Arrowshaft has had its ups and downs, but always remember, these two men presided over some big hit games that put us on the map."

Arguments and objections broke out among the shocked employees. Romero raised her arms to regain everyone's attention.

"Mr. Magowan will be joining a venture capital firm down in Austin, and Mr. Seabury, as I understand it, will be running a startup in Seattle. That leaves me, your human resource manager, in charge."

Incoherent expressions of disbelief spread through the assembly.

Romero grinned. She was starting to enjoy her performance. "It's like that old song, right? Ain't that a kick in the head?"

The group seemed to catch her spirit. They cheered.

"Yeah, thanks for the support. But I won't be running things for very long. Maybe for another minute or so, until I introduce our new boss, Donald Bakstrom."

The employees gasped. Romero raised her hands again.

"Now calm down. This kind of upheaval, it's a lot to swallow in one day, I grant you. Let me say that Don comes to us from a very successful tenure at Brass Knuckles, where he led teams to build a number of hit mobile games. No doubt many of you have played *Shrine of the Sword* on your smartphones. I know I have."

A lean man in a T-shirt and cargo shorts marched up to the podium. Romero stretched out an arm in his direction.

"And here he is, folks. Don Bakstrom, ready to lead us onward and upward. Let's make some noise for our new CEO."

Scattered clapping marked the lean man's arrival at the lectern.

"Hello, everyone. Onward and upward sounds kind of vague, don't you think? The real reason I'm here is to stop the backward and downward. This company has a legacy of distinguished titles, and I'm proud to join up and continue the tradition. Together we're going to set the online banking world on fire, and *PieceMakers* — well, it follows your biggest hit. All we need to do is get that puppy out the door. And that, friends — I hope we'll be friends — is what I know how to do. So . . . stand by me, and Arrowshaft will . . ."

" . . . blah blah blah," said Page to no one in particular. He was standing in the middle of the crowd, as stunned by developments

as the rest of his co-workers. He turned away from his former em-
ployer and pushed through the crush to the exit. He was sure no
one would bring in a guy like Bakstrom except as a caretaker. The
man's appointment was proof that the company was circling the
drain. When it would actually gurgle down the tubes, that was the
only question.

▼

An hour later, Page was sitting on the loading dock outside the
company warehouse, dangling his legs over the rubber bumpers,
sipping a cup of bad coffee and thinking about his glorious tenure
as a shipping clerk. While he was contemplating life, a UPS truck
backed up to deliver the latest load of video game merchandise. The
driver was new.

"Hey, there," he called out, "this here Arrowshaft?"

Page shrugged. "I think so. For a few more weeks, maybe."

"Got a lot of boxes for you. Sign for me?"

"I'm no longer authorized," Page replied. "I don't work here anymore."

The UPS man shook his head and proceeded to deposit large
cardboard boxes on the dock. Then he presented his manifest to
Page.

"Look — I don't care if you're homeless. Just sign already, got a
busy day ahead."

Page relented and scribbled his name on the dotted line.

"Thanks, pal. Have a nice life."

Page hardly heard the man. His thoughts were drifting far away
until they were interrupted by a voice from within.

"Yoo-hoo, Ollie . . . you there?"

Page ducked back inside to find Vivian Romero standing by the
department's workbench.

"Hi, Viv, great pep talk this morning."

"You're hilarious, Ollie."

Page put on a lopsided grin. "I don't see you down here very often. What's up?"

"I just wanted to give you a personal briefing. You know, the situation, the outlook, all the corporate craziness . . ."

"You don't have to, I'm hip. I worked for that asshole Bakstrom at Brass Knuckles. I know why he's here."

"Well, then . . ."

Page lifted a box from the bench and held it up to demonstrate his resignation.

"My stuff."

"I see."

Page reached into the box and hauled out a soldering iron.

"I'm liberating this thing. Spoils of war."

"I won't tell."

He reached in again and produced one of the department's industrial tape dispensers.

"And I'm taking this as a souvenir."

"Bravo."

Romero impulsively wrapped Page in a motherly hug.

"You're a good kid, Ollie. Take care of yourself."

Page noticed moisture glistening in Romero's eyes. He surmised that some of the sentiment was for him, and some for the disintegration of Arrowshaft, which he currently represented.

"What about you?" he inquired.

Romero waved nonchalantly.

"Oh, I'll be joining Doyle down in Austin."

"Austin? Texas?"

"We have a history. Got to keep that man organized."

"Wow, I didn't know."

48
00110000

Page's garage seemed more claustrophobic than usual after two weeks of constant occupancy. His only relief from the walls closing in were trips to the market for basic supplies and to pizza joints for take-out food.

He remembered his anxiety over money when he first arrived in California, and between TV binges he began to worry about his bank balance again.

He fired up his smartphone and composed a message:

> *Hi Gram, hope you're well —*
>
> *Just finished up my job @ Arrowshaft. You were right about video games. Tough, but I'm tough too. Taking some time to look around now. Expecting opportunity to knock soon. If not, I'll definitely be home 4 Xmas.*
>
> *xoxo — OP*

He considered adding his mother to the address line, but decided against it, fearing a hysterically negative reaction. Or worse, none at all.

He tapped the *Send* button, then racked his bike onto the trunk of his old Honda and headed for Mount Burdell.

The arduous grind up the steep incline shifted his mind into meditation mode. The higher he pedaled, the more he liked the idea of resuming his stock boy job at Feldman's Home Improvement Center. A safe haven while he looked for better possibilities.

Up on top, Page laid his bike on the brown grass and sat down cross-legged beside it.

His mind turned first to Brava Erpenstock, to the conundrum of a beautiful woman who was not the virtuous maiden his fantasies imagined so vividly. Then his thoughts tumbled sideways to consider Emilee DuFrayne, whose friendship masqueraded as bitterness. He was slowly grasping the astonishing idea that, underneath the rough sarcasm, she had eyes for him, the ultimate clueless geek. His head drooped onto his chest. What a dope . . . he never learned how to read her, and he still didn't know how to read himself.

Damn.

In Real Life, Page acknowledged ruefully, there were no save-games to load and refight a battle, no buttons to push and start over.

To rescue himself from painful self-criticism he turned a hopeful eye to the scenery.

The view to the south and east was sharply spectacular on this early autumn day. The air was warm and dry, and the scent of oaks and madrone trees was intoxicating. No fog obscured the bay. Out on the water he could see the long wake of a catamaran ferry speeding toward Vallejo. No clouds hid the blue tints of Mount Tamalpais, the sleeping lady looming over Marin County. Light traffic along the freeway far below his lookout traced a wavy line through the higgledy-piggledy real estate developments of Novato. In the middle distance, turkey vultures were cruising back and forth along the lower slopes he had just ascended, dipping their wings erratically to catch every zephyr.

He could feel himself relaxing, feel his cares evaporating. He opened up his fanny pack and extracted a well-chilled beer.

Then his phone rang. He killed the incoming call and silenced the ringer.

"Here's to California," he said. He raised the bottle toward the world at his feet and downed a prodigious swig.

▼

He was on his way back down the mountain, bouncing bravely over roots and rocks, when his phone vibrated urgently. He ignored it. Then, a few hairpin turns further downhill, it vibrated again. He ignored it again. In the parking lot, as he was getting ready to hoist his bike onto his car, it vibrated a third time.

"Christ . . ." he muttered at the technological irritant interrupting his pastoral afternoon.

He stabbed at the answer button.

"Page here . . ."

"Jesus, Ollie, where you been? I've been calling and calling."

"Karen? You sound stressed. My phone's on buzz, I might have missed you. Where's the fire?"

"Our game is on fire. We're in review at Apple and Google. Fingers crossed for approval on both mobile systems in about a week."

"Oh good, that's good. Glad to hear it."

"Contain your enthusiasm for another minute or so. I've got news."

Hoffman's voice conveyed a sly smile. It put Page on guard.

"What kind of news . . ?"

"Listen up, doofus — *Expanding Universe Entertainment,* where I work my day job, has bought Arrowshaft's intellectual property out of bankruptcy. Know what that means?"

"Uhh . . . nope, not really."

"It means they now own *PieceMakers* and *Money Matters 360.* They're going to finish both projects. It means they need programmers. It means you, Oliver Page, have just landed a new job."

"You're kidding."

"Meet me tonight at Puerto Seguro for details."

Before Page could ask any of the dozen questions that popped into his head, Hoffman rang off.

▼

It was dark when Page arrived at Puerto Seguro. He approached the restaurant entrance apprehensively. He couldn't wrap his head around Karen Hoffman's apparently friendly job offer, because she had good reason to hate him. After all, he had just turned her boy-friend over to the feds.

He stood in the doorway for a long moment, ducking his head under the festive *papel picado* banners hung on long strings beneath the ceiling. He cautiously surveyed the booths, estimating the possibility of some ugly surprise.

But no, there was Hoffman, leaning out from behind a seat back, waving cheerfully.

He sidled over — five long steps — and abruptly took a couple of long steps backward.

Sitting opposite Hoffman was Jimmy Fillmore. He grinned at the effect he was having on his former friend.

"Hello, Ollie," he said.

Page blanched. He turned and hastily retreated toward the exit.

"Hey, you dope, come back here," called Hoffman.

Page turned around to face his ex-partners.

"Oh man . . . Jimmy . . . out on bail or something?"

Hoffman beckoned energetically to summon Page back to the table. He warily returned to face the pair.

Fillmore stood, reached out for Page's hand, pumped it vigorously, and used his grip to drag Page toward a seat. He was grinning from ear to ear.

"Hey, bro. All is forgiven. Siddown. Join us."

Page reluctantly slid into the seat beside Hoffman.

"Geez, Karen . . . why didn't you tell me? What's the trap for?"

"We didn't think you'd show."

"I wouldn't have."

Hoffman nodded. "Tell him, Jaybird."

Fillmore grinned again. "I'm not out on bail."

"Mmm. What do they call it? Own recognizance?"

"Nope."

"Did you plead? They're letting you off?"

Fillmore swirled the residue of a margarita around in its glass.

"I will pay a fine."

Page started to relax. "Whoa, that's good. No trial, right? No jail?"

"None of the above, my friend."

Hoffman was bouncing in her chair. She couldn't contain herself through the slow Q-and-A any longer and cut to the chase:

"He's joining the NSA."

Page was flabbergasted. He slapped his forehead.

"No effing way!"

Fillmore spread his hands wide. "Way, bro. The same dudes you set on me offered the job. I'm moving to Baltimore, where I will hook up with those boys as an analyst specializing in the latest hacker cracks — procedurally generated one-time pads."

"After we ship, whenever that happens, I'll be moving too," added Hoffman.

"Holy crap!" marveled Page.

"You heard it, you know it. Turns out you did me a big favor."

A pitcher of margaritas arrived at the table. They filled their glasses and clicked them together.

"Here's to . . . something or other," said Page.

49
00110001

Page's new job involved just about the same commute as his old one: a trip on the SMART train from Petaluma to the Hamilton Field Station in Novato, and then, varying from his previous routine, a short bike ride to the former military airport itself. The Expanding Universe offices were in a new building beside the runway designed to look like the hangars of old.

On his first day he was greeted by Leo Thorpe and Vitus Lozoraitis, ex-Arrowshaft employees like himself.

"Yo, Page. Welcome to the projects that will not die."

"Thanks. This is all very weird, huh?"

"Video game development," said Thorpe with a crooked grin, "makes weird look normal."

Lozoraitis handed Page a sheaf of papers.

"Here you go, Leo's design dox. Karen told me you two have built a game, and you coded up all the enemy AI."

"Aggrozoids?"

"Got a version I can play?"

Page handed him his smartphone with the game running. Lozoraitis was quickly absorbed in eliminating an alien horde that was scuttling toward him across the office floor. Page looked on in suspense. What if his new boss thought it was junk?

Sure enough, pretty soon a deep frown creased Lozoraitis' forehead. Page's heart sank.

A couple of minutes later, Lozoraitis pressed the pause button and looked up from the screen. His frown was gone.

"Is this build running in your sandbox?"

"That's the published version. We're out there."

"How's it doing?"

Page cracked an ironic smile. "We're making money, thanks to some viral advertising Karen's partner set up."

Lozoraitis handed the phone to Thorpe, who spent a few moments quietly blasting another swarm of monsters.

Page was terrified of the silence, fearing the worst.

But then . . .

"Gotta say, your attack patterns are pretty good," said Thorpe.

Lozoraitis grinned and rubbed his hands together. "Awesome! I guess Karen knew what she was talking about. So, here's the plan . . . we think you should warm up by plugging your AI code into *PieceMakers.*"

This compliment, coming from a veteran lead programmer, made Page blush. He breathed an enormous sigh of relief.

"Sure, I'll get on it. Who else is here from Arrowshaft?"

Thorpe chuckled. "You're looking at us. Oh, except we hired a marketing company. Ready? Take a look at *Adweek* . . ."

Thorpe clicked a bookmark on his web browser and showed Page the link:

STARTUP TO MAXIMIZE AD VALUE

High Beam Consulting, a newly formed Seattle company, is making waves online, advising a growing list of clients on the most efficient way to spend their limited advertising and marketing money. Ben Seabury, CEO, and his partner, Brava Erpenstock, Creative Director, are passionate about their take on the biz.

"We think companies, especially those who lack constant presence in the marketplace, like video game publishers, will benefit from our analysis of media opportunities," declares Erpenstock. "We're already seeing a lot of success, for our clients and for ourselves."

"Erpenstock . . ." muttered Page.

"Yeah, her and Seabury," said Thorpe with a wink that confused the new hire.

"What . . ?"

"Vitus and I have been speculating for months. We were pretty sure those two were an item. Now we know."

"Now we know," echoed Page with a dull nod.

Just before lunch, Karen Hoffman conducted Page to his new desk in the Expanding Universe cube farm.

"Think of each cubicle as a star in the galaxy," said Hoffman.

"You can't be serious," sighed Page, scrutinizing the waist-high walls of the tiny workspace he was expected to occupy.

"I'm not. Working conditions are grim, but I just quoted the official description on the Spandex recruitment posters."

Page took a seat, swiveled around in his chair.

"I'll live. I'm a programmer now — beats shipping Devil Heads."

Hoffman studied her young friend, the accurately self-described clueless geek. Yup, geek. Yup, clueless.

"By the way . . ." she said, wondering how best to break some news even as she was breaking it. ". . . I ran into Emilee DuFrayne the other day."

Page's chest tightened.

"Uh-oh," he stammered, turning pale. "Why tell me?"

"She asked about you."

"Really — ?"

"Doesn't mean she wants to see you."

"Probably not. But . . . I should check. Where is she?"

"Working at the Butterfly. One of the baristas."

Page jumped out of his chair and directed his long legs toward the exit.

"I think she referred to you as *Dumbo,*" warned Hoffman.

Page didn't hear her. He was already inside the down elevator, and the doors were closing.

▼

Page was nervous entering the Butterfly, even though he was a familiar face to the staff. Well, familiar to the staff he was familiar with. DuFrayne? A barista? That was something new.

He ordered coffee at the counter — doppio cappuccino — and eased over to the stupendous *La Marzocco* espresso maker. It was big enough to hide behind, and he spent a few moments using its bulk to stay hidden from the operator. He could just see the top of her head bobbing around as she prepared his drink. Soon, however, with what appeared to be practiced efficiency, his coffee was ready. A hand slid the cup onto the counter beside the espresso maker. Page moved to pick it up, and there was DuFrayne staring at him.

"Hey, Duffy . . ." he ventured.

"Hey, Page," she replied, already busy with another order.

Page sipped his coffee, savoring the aroma and the bitter tang with satisfaction.

"Good cappuccino, Duff."

"Thanks."

"I just heard you were over here."

"Yeah, who told you?"

"Karen Hoffman, why?"

"That bitch, fuck her."

Page ignored the gripe.

"You know, I tried to call you. Um, repeatedly. You never picked up. Never called back."

"No, Arrowshaft . . . Arrowshaft people . . . rear-view mirror, man."

Page scratched his head uneasily.

"I never got the idea about things — you, me — until you left."

"Yes, you are a dunce."

"I'm sorry."

"Don't be. Move on. That's what I'm doing."

Page balanced on the balls of his feet. He stuck his free hand in a pocket. He was about to do something he had never done before — ask for a date. The idea made him feel numb all over.

"Well ... what I'd like to do, if you'd be interested is ... maybe ... maybe have dinner somewhere."

DuFrayne froze. Her grey eyes fastened on the jittery young man before her like gunsights targeting vermin.

Page caught the anger behind her steely gaze.

"We could go to Grazella right here in town," he said, hoping to defuse the unexpected hostility.

She continued to regard him coldly.

"Or, how about that Chinese place you mentioned, up the road?"

DuFrayne folded her arms.

"You're asking me for what? A date?"

Page fidgeted with his cappuccino.

"I guess so, if people, you know, date anymore."

"A fucking *date.*"

"Um, yeah. We should get together. You're the only friend I ever made at Arrowshaft. I could always talk to you."

"A date..." repeated DuFrayne in tones of contempt. She shook her head.

"Yeah."

"I had a crush on you," she confessed. "No idea why, you're such a dope. And you never noticed."

"I was after those hackers." He shrugged sheepishly. "Distracted."

"So now you want a *date,*" she growled. "Tell you what, *Dumbo* — fuck you."

Page rocked back on his heels. He could not process what he was hearing.

"Whoa, there. It took a while, but I woke up ... let's forget Arrowshaft, the damn boxes, the tape, those stupid labels, and go from now."

"Second that. Go from now. Drink your coffee and get lost."

"Come on, Duff, what's wrong? What did I do?"

"Nothing. That's the point. So — know what? Go fuck yourself. Or find some geek-chick who likes retards. I'm over that phase."

Page was in a state of shock. Each word out of DuFrayne's mouth battered his psyche like a physical blow. His skin was burning with humiliating shame. He could not think of a thing to say, could not marshal any argument to advance his cause.

He deposited his half-empty coffee cup on the counter with a shaky hand and stumbled to the door.

DuFrayne didn't bother to watch him go.

"So long, dipshit," she muttered and whipped up the next customer's espresso with flying fingers.

▼

Back in the Expanding Universe office, Page sat down at the desk in his little cubicle and wrote an email message:

Hi there, Gram & Mom & Charles:

Latest news — great new job, making lots of friends, keeping the rent under 25% of my amazing salary if you include money from my indie game.

That's right, we're a hit, so tell all your friends to play Aggrozoid Defenders on their phones. (I know you won't, it's okay.)

Apologies — very busy, so another Xmas out west, I'm afraid. Don't worry about me. My oil is changed, tires all rotated.

xoxo — OP

50
00110010

Page was slow to settle into his new job at Expanding Universe. Every now and then his programming mind was hijacked by fugitive thoughts of Brava Erpenstock — yes, even now after all he knew about her — and flooded by regrets over the months he spent working with Emilee DuFrayne. To compensate, he got into the habit of taking an early train into work and a late one home. It was the only way he could get anything done.

On this crisp morning in early November he hopped aboard the SMART car in Petaluma and hooked his bike up for the trip. He noticed that the only other two-wheeler on the train, a fancy carbon-fiber road bike, had a lime green helmet dangling from the handlebars.

He walked forward through the car, looking for a window seat where he could plug in his laptop and check his email. Halfway along, just past the snack bar, he spotted the young red-haired woman whose bike he had seen. She was sitting with her back to him, holding up her smartphone, playing a mobile game on it. She was cackling to herself as she blasted numerous small critters into extinction.

Page stopped beside her.

"Good morning," he said.

She looked up from her game.

"Oh hello," she replied. "It's you" — she grinned — "the would-be racer I always crush."

Page shrugged, silently admitting his inferior riding skills. He pointed at her phone.

"You play?"

She nodded and fumbled for the pause button.

"Yup."

"What's the game, if you don't mind my asking?"

She clicked on a button that brought her view back to the splash screen and held the phone up for Page to see.

"*Aggrozoid Defenders.* It's new."

Page pursed his lips.

"Any good?"

She giggled. "Really cool. Little aliens are running right along the floor here on the train. Augmented reality, right? And I'm stopping them from killing me and taking over the world. You should try it."

Page spread his hands apart.

"Uhh . . . that's my game you're playing. I designed it."

"You what . . !?"

"Yeah, it's an indie project. Developed it with a couple of my friends."

The woman laughed.

"Shut up!"

"It's true. I'm a game developer."

The woman, who Page decided was rather attractive, dropped the phone into her lap. She knitted her hands behind her head and regarded the young man standing by her seat. She remembered running across him from time to time without paying much attention. Now she gave him a good once-over. He was tall, gangly, with a reedy voice, and he was kind of good-looking in an indescribably innocent sort of way.

She picked up the phone and waved it at him.

"You really made this? No lie?"

"I really did. If you get tired of the aliens, you can switch them out for zombies."

"Well, I'll be damned."

Page took a breath, exhaled, and somehow found the courage to make an introduction. He stuck out his hand.

"I'm Oliver Page. What's your name?"

"Linda Yost."

She took his hand and shook it.

"Where are you working now? I heard Arrowshaft closed, huh?"

"I'm over at Expanding Universe, in one of the fake-o hangars. We're finishing Arrowshaft's final projects."

Yost fluffed her red hair.

"Sounds like you landed on your feet."

"Lucky break."

"They happen. Now you don't have to bike as far. In a sprint, you might be able to beat me."

Page waggled his head ruefully. "Maybe, but probably not."

This short discussion exhausted Page's conversational repertory. He looked around the train, desperately trying to imagine some further topic of interest.

"They say it might rain tomorrow," offered Yost, as bereft of conversational gambits as himself. Her willingness to resort to weather talk sent a tiny social signal.

"Say," he said, pointing across the car. "There's a coffee shop right over there. Buy you a latte?"

11792950R00155

Made in the USA
San Bernardino, CA
07 December 2018